THE DOV

The Dove Stone

P. S. Daunton

Dernier Publishing
London

Copyright © P. S. Daunton 2022
Published by Dernier Publishing
P.O. Box 793, Orpington, BR6 1FA, England
www.dernierpublishing.com

First edition.

ISBN: 978-1-912457-51-9

Scriptures and additional materials quoted are from the Good News
Bible © 1994 published by the Bible Societies/HarperCollins
Publishers Ltd UK, Good News Bible © American Bible Society
1966, 1971, 1976, 1992. Used with permission.

For my family, whose unceasing encouragement
helped me to persevere.

Acknowledgements

My thanks go to Janet and Andrew Wilson, whose professional editing has informed my writing.

Also to the children of Samlesbury Church of England Primary School, who gave up their time to help me.

Author's Note

Asterisked words and phrases* are explained in the Glossary at the back of the book.

Where is *The Dove Stone* Set?

This book is set in Lancashire, which is a county in the north of England. It is rugged and wild in places. There are areas where you still need a compass and a map, or you will get lost up on the boggy moors.

The Romans built an important garrison* here as a way-station for men and supplies going north to build Hadrian's Wall*. They built it by the great River Ribble which the Romans called Belisama* after a goddess.

The Dove Stone is set by the River Ribble at the end of the 5th century, after the Romans left Britain. The land was occupied at that time by the Brigantes* people. Very little is recorded about this period in history, so it is ideal for an imaginative story.

Who Were the Brigantes* People?

When the Romans decided to abandon Britain, the soldiers simply followed orders, packed up their belongings and departed. They left behind everything they couldn't carry. Large numbers of local people had been employed by the Romans and they, too, were abandoned. In Lancashire, the local people were called the Brigantes.

Where Did the Brigantes Live?

Once the Romans left, some people would have colonised the abandoned garrisons. Others would have drifted away to form smaller settlements in places where the land was good to farm.

We don't know what these new settlements looked like, but they probably had a wooden fence around them for protection from wild animals and thieves.

How Did They Live?

It is likely that settlements would have been cooperatives of farmers. The more prosperous ones would have had a blacksmith, a carpenter and a leatherman*, as these were essential skills for the survival of a community at that time.

Families would have built longhouses* to live in but we don't really know what they would have looked like, as no historical evidence remains.

What Did They Eat?

Hunting and farming were the main ways of supplying food for the community. Rivers would have been a source of fish, and the woods would have had wild boar*, deer and rabbits to hunt. People also supplemented their diet with pigeons and doves, and cows would have been kept for milk.

In this story I've imagined people with a pike* and dogs so they can both hunt, and defend themselves. I've placed allotments* outside the settlement fence, where crops could be grown.

Who Else Lived Here?

The early church grew throughout the Roman Empire, following the death of Jesus. We know there were Christian believers working on Hadrian's Wall, who would have passed through Lancashire to get there.

These may have been led by monks.* In this period, monks sometimes spent time in solitary places, so they could devote themselves to quiet prayer and meditation.

Jesus said to them, "When you pray, say this:
'Father: May your holy name be honoured;
may your Kingdom come.
Give us day by day the food we need.
Forgive us our sins,
for we forgive everyone who does us wrong.
And do not bring us to hard testing.'"

Luke 11:2-4

CONTENTS

ONE

Lost!

Wolf's silver fur shone in the moonlight. Lifting his muzzle, he sniffed the damp air. A faint smell of the river mingled on the breeze. He pricked up his ears, listening to the changing sounds as night gave way to dawn. His sharp eyes made out the shiny snake of the river which lay before them in the bottom of the valley. He turned to Rhiannon as he caught the faint reassuring howl of Juniper in the settlement, and knew at once the direction of home.

Rhiannon shivered as she pulled her old woollen cloak closer, a finger sliding over the red enamel of the circular pin* at her neck. The howl was far beyond her hearing. She eased back her shoulders, which were stiff from the night she'd spent in the hollow of a tree. Wolf's wet nose nuzzled

1

her hand, bringing a smile to her weary face. Gently she stroked his head and ruffled his ears. She was totally lost. "Which way now?" she asked him, straining her eyes to see in the darkness.

Suddenly, a twig snapped behind them and Rhiannon whirled round. Wide-eyed she stood there, straining her ears to listen, her heart pounding in her chest and her hand on the hilt of her knife. A rat scurried through the undergrowth and she sighed with relief. "It's just a rat," she told Wolf.

Slowly, Wolf led the way down the steep wooded slope towards the river, the wet grass soaking his long fur. Rhiannon slithered and slid along behind him. "Belisama only helps in the light," she worried. "Now she'll be gathering souls in the darkness, sucking them down into the river's black heart. We have to cross the river to get home! But how are we going to find the crossing in the dark?" She yanked at the edge of her cloak, pulling it from brambles as she passed, adding to the snags in the fabric. Wolf waited, his bushy tail twitching impatiently, until she caught up with him.

"But we can't wait for the light, we have to get back before the gates open," Rhiannon worried, rubbing impatiently at the mud on her soft leather breeches. "It's all well and good Torsa saying there are fat rabbits on this side of the river. We didn't find any!"

Wolf slipped quickly under the branch that hung across their path. Rhiannon shoved it out of her way letting it twang back as she passed, splattering the earth with drops of rain that had been held amongst the leaves. "At dawn the gates will open and I'll have to explain why I didn't get home. They'll be worrying about me."

The valley bottom was even darker than it had been up on the hill. Wolf padded ahead, sniffing the ground as he went; his ears up and his nose absorbed in the search for the stepping stones to cross the river. The day before they had crossed safely in the light, leaving their scent on the grass, if Wolf could only find it. Then there it was! He stood rock steady, his nose pointing to the first stepping stone.

"You've found the crossing!" Rhiannon cried out in relief, stumbling towards him. Once they were over the river Belisama couldn't hurt them; they would be back in their homelands and safe. But first they had to persuade the river goddess to let them cross in the dark.

Rhiannon stared at the crossing, fear gripping her stomach. The river was in full spate after the previous night's rain, and was rippling over the tops of the stones. Rhiannon and Wolf looked silently at each other but there was no choice – the crossing had to be made. "I should have brought my pike!" Rhiannon whispered.

Her foot slithered on the slippery surface as she stepped on to the first stone. She licked her dry lips; she could barely see the far side of the bank. She took a small piece of iron in the shape of a hazel nut from the pocket* on her belt, and closed her eyes. "Please Belisama," she pleaded, "take this nut and leave us to make the crossing, just as you promised to our forefathers." She bent down and placed the nut carefully against the furthest edge of the first stone. Then she waited.

Wolf's tail twitched. The gurgling river sucked at the stones. Rhiannon turned as a screeching owl flew behind

3

them. But when she looked back the nut was gone. "Good," she thought, stepping confidently onto the second stone and placing a new hazel nut against its edge.

Wolf mastered the stone behind her, then they waited, listening to the churning call of the river around the stones. A silver fish leaped up clear of the surface slapping back into the water startling them both. "That nut's gone too," she told Wolf as she moved on again.

By the time they reached the middle stone, both banks had almost disappeared into the shadows, leaving nothing but the seething water around them. They stood silently waiting for the nut to be taken. The river whispered to them as it flowed past, calling them to slide within its watery grasp.

Rhiannon fiddled with the pin at her throat, forcing down the panic in her chest. "Oh Leon," she thought, "I could use your help right now." She wished she could see her older brother waving from the far bank, pleased to find her safe. But the nut was still there.

The river sang its song of death. Gurgling and gargling as it rushed by her feet, it mesmerised her with its twinkling. Wolf let out a long, low growl. Rhiannon trembled as she almost lost her balance for a moment, but the nut was gone.

She stepped on to the next stone as the clouds parted, bathing her in moonlight. She turned her face towards the sky, her stomach a pit of dread. "Please Belisama," she prayed, "please help us home."

But it seemed Belisama was not pleased. A screaming black crow flew across the river from the trees and crashed into the back of Rhiannon's head, knocking her forwards.

4

She flailed her arms as the crow pulled at her thick plait, its wings flapping round her face. Rhiannon's feet slipped; she felt herself losing her balance. Wolf bayed from the rock behind her, jumping with the force of each bark, but there was nothing he could do. She slithered off the stone, and cried out as she fell into the water with a splash. Her breath froze in her throat as the cold water grabbed her and pulled her down.

Wolf howled in panic; turning round and round on his stone. Rhiannon clawed for the stone's edge as the force of the river dragged her away downstream. She kicked frantically, but her mouth filled up with foam as she slipped below the surface.

She stared up at Wolf as she rose in the water. Water went up her nose; the pain in her chest was crushing. "No!" she screamed, as she saw Wolf jump towards her into the waiting river. Cold helplessness smothered her as she saw Wolf being dragged downstream, and she was sucked below the surface of the water once more.

Suddenly she felt a strong hand grab the back of her jerkin. She was lifted out of the tumult, dragged towards the shore and deposited on dry ground. Shivering, spluttering and coughing, she lay still until she could breathe more freely. She turned to her rescuer but the strange brown-robed figure was already running down the river bank, his outline etched in the moonlight.

Gradually Rhiannon got to her knees and then to her feet, shivering with a cold that froze her bones. "Who is that man?" she wondered. She stood for a moment swaying as she looked back across the stones – then she remembered.

Terror rose up in her throat. "Wolf," she cried out in anguish, "where are you?" And then, overwhelmed and exhausted, she crumpled to the ground.

TWO

Saving Wolf

The sun peered over the tall picket fence of the main yard, warming the cold ground beyond the long shadows. A skinny boy, with a bronze torc* around his neck was standing by the gate. Leaning on his pike, he stood next to Maelbrigte, Rhiannon's mother. His breeches bagged over his knees where the fabric was worn thin and a dirty toe poked though the leather of his tatty shoe.

"Surely it's time to open these?" Maelbrigte muttered. She tossed her head angrily towards the stout, wooden gates, which were locked together by a thick bar across their middle. Doran nodded in agreement.

Rhiannon was his friend and he liked her mother – but she also intimidated him. Maelbrigte had earned his respect

7

when she'd taught them all to fight – she was a good teacher.

"She didn't return," Maelbrigte told him with a frown. "Rhiannon didn't come home before the gates were shut last night."

"She stayed out all night?" Doran gasped, his heart thumping in his chest. He couldn't quite take it in. How could Rhiannon be so reckless? The men stayed out on hunting trips but they were both too young to do that. What could have happened?

Maelbrigte's fingers picked nervously at the enamelled pin that held in place her fur-lined cloak, which was draped over her shoulders and her long, grey plait. "Silfor has gone to tell Governor Erdig and to gather some men for a search," she said, with a catch in her voice. "We didn't miss her until this morning. I thought she was with Miriam. There's been talk of a stranger in the woods ..."

Maelbrigte pulled herself to her full height as the gatekeeper approached. A group of men was forming in front of the longhouse behind them. "About time," she snapped angrily, her body taut with fear.

Doran's eyes met the gatekeeper's anxious frown as he ran forward to help with the gates. Together they strained to push the bolt bar as the deep growl of the long horn* split the air, announcing that the gates were opening.

Slowly, the bar moved, grumbling against the iron awls*. When the bar was nearly home, the old gates began to open gradually by themselves – and a sodden, cloaked figure fell back against the cold ground. Doran stared in disbelief as

Wolf slid next to Rhiannon's body and on to the dark earth. At first no one moved.

Then Silfor, who had just arrived, rushed across the yard and dropped to his knees by his daughter. Maelbrigte knelt beside him and took Rhiannon's icy hand in her own. "We need to get her warm," she said. Silfor tenderly stroked back his daughter's dark hair, put his ear close to her mouth and listened. "She's breathing," was his only comment.

Doran breathed a sigh of relief. "May Belisama be praised," he whispered. "She's still with us." A small group of villagers formed around the little group. Silfor lifted his daughter into his muscular arms, leaving her wet cloak still half covering the motionless dog. Without another word, he and Maelbrigte hurried up the road between the wooden longhouses towards their home.

Doran sniffed as he watched them leave, wiping his nose on his unwashed sleeve. He watched as the gatekeeper made sure the gates were fully open and secured. Then as the crowd returned to their chores, he sidled over to Wolf and stroked him gently. Rhiannon would be taken care of by her parents, but what about Wolf?

"Well, they're not too worried about you," he said, leaning over the dog and listening for his breath. The dog's fur was cold, and matted with river weed, but his chest was warm and Doran felt the faintest pulse.

A small blonde boy skipped across the yard towards them and leaned over Doran. "Is Wolf dead?" Nico asked as he snuggled against his brother.

"No, he's not dead, but we need to take care of him," Doran replied. "He and Rhiannon must have fallen in the

9

river. Maelbrigte and Silfor have taken Rhiannon home to get her warm." With difficulty he picked up the dog and looked down at his younger brother. "Bring the pike. We'll have to fish later."

The two boys walked to their hut at the far edge of the group of longhouses. Doran struggled with his heavy burden, and shivered as Wolf's cold, wet fur soaked his own tunic. Nico skipped beside him, tossing Doran's smooth wooden pike from hand to hand.

Inside the hut, three beds of deer hide hung from the wall, ready to be taken down at night. A wooden trestle table*, with a few bowls and cups on top, stood to one side of the central fire. The only light came from the doorway, while smoke from the fire clouded the air.

The fire was dying, smothered by the wet logs Nico had heaped upon it. Doran sighed. "One day, Nico, you will learn to make sure the wood is dry first." He knelt down, placing Wolf on the dry earth near the embers, and poked the fire with a wooden stick. He blew at the faint orange glow, coaxing it alight. Slowly, the fire began to crackle and burn, giving out a healing warmth.

Doran began stroking out the river water from Wolf's fur, willing life to return. Thin curls of smoke floated toward the ceiling, chasing the rats that lived amongst the muddied branches of the roof. They scurried about unnoticed in the brushwood, knocking small bits of moss down to the ground below.

All morning the two boys stayed in the hut, watching Wolf while he slept. When at last he stirred, Doran nursed him with milk and water, wiping the grime from around his eyes. Nico leaned over him, watching. Doran smiled, proud to have saved such a valuable animal.

When the sun rose high in the sky, Wolf raised his head, then got to his feet. "At last," Doran said, as he felt the dog's chest heave with a large intake of breath. "I think you're going to make it."

"Shall we take him back home now?" Nico asked.

Doran shook his head. "They'll be too busy worrying about Rhiannon. I'll take him later. He can stay with us for now." Doran's stomach growled. "I'm hungry. We'd better go and check the traps." Nico smiled up adoringly at his older brother then buried his face in Wolf's thick fur.

Doran blinked in the sunlight as they left the gloomy hut. Wolf padded slowly beside him while Nico skipped on ahead. After leaving the gate, they made their way around the edge of the thirty longhouses of the settlement. The disordered cluster was at the highest point in the valley, surrounded by a high wooden fence of pointed logs which protected their homes. They headed towards the wide dirt path which wove gently down the slope to the allotments, then towards the river and the woods.

Doran slowed his pace to keep next to the dog. Wolf limped along, sniffing at the grass but noticing little. Every now and then he paused and lent against Doran's leg as if he was taking strength from him.

"Morning!" Miriam called as she walked up the slope towards them, her hoe* resting over her shoulder. Miriam was Rhiannon's best friend. Doran looked up and smiled.

"We're looking after Wolf," Nico stated importantly, hopping from one foot to the other then taking hold of

11

Miriam's hand. "Have you got any food?"

"So you've heard about Rhiannon?" she said to them both, her eyes shining with the gossip. "I'm so relieved she's all right." The light breeze fluttered the curly hair around her pretty face. She looked down at Nico. "So you're hungry?"

Nico grinned up at her, hopefully. Doran nodded his permission, and Nico skipped happily back to the settlement with Miriam.

Doran knelt down and ruffled Wolf's ears. He looked steadily into the dog's tired eyes. "It's just me and you to check the traps, then," he said, his stomach growling again.

Doran had set his rabbit traps in the woodland that covered the eastern slope of the hill, but as they came to the beech copse they stopped, and Doran's heart sank into his boots. Torsa was standing in the middle of the ring of trees, watching his big black hound gobble down a fat rabbit. Doran ground his teeth. That was his rabbit, from his trap!

Torsa's hands rested lightly on his hips. From behind he looked like the great warrior his late father had been. The strong leather straps from his sword belt crossed between his broad shoulder blades – although no sword hung from it, as he had yet to earn the right to own a sword. His blonde hair wound around the huge silver torc he wore at his neck. Suddenly, Pilot stopped eating. He pointed his bloodied nose towards Doran and growled, pulling back his thick lips and showing his great white teeth. Torsa turned and his shoulders heaved as he started to laugh. "Oh, look who it is!"

For one second Doran thought about running, but Pilot's stare staked him to the spot. The enormous dog began to walk slowly towards him, snarling and growling. His pointed ears were flat to his skull and his huge paws crushed the grass where he stepped. Pilot had a bad reputation and Doran swallowed hard. His throat felt dry. No one would hear his call for help from there.

"Were those your traps?" Torsa asked mockingly, holding up the three rabbits he'd tied together with twine. "And you saved the dog!" he said with a sneer, noticing Wolf. "Only you've wasted your time on a woman's whelp." He spat on the ground in front of Wolf. Wolf cowered, lowering his head in submission to the bigger dog. He was too weak to fight today.

Doran's legs began to shake and sweat trickled slowly down his spine. "Those are my traps," he stuttered.

"And I've emptied them! We'll have rabbit stew and you will have . . . nothing!"

Doran gritted his teeth. Torsa smiled, throwing the rabbits on to the ground in front of Pilot. "Wait!" he said firmly to the dog, while still looking at Doran. The dog left them, but drool dripped from his jowls.

Anger rose up in Doran's chest, but there was nothing he could do. Torsa strode forward and took hold of the front of Doran's shabby jerkin, lifting him up onto his toes. Doran's torc dug into his throat, cutting off his breath as Torsa pushed his fingers hard underneath it.

"You think you can impress Maelbrigte then, do you?" he sneered. "By saving a dog!" Doran's head began to feel groggy. Fear crushed his heart and he thought he was going to faint. Then Torsa let go of the torc and Doran fell to the ground, gasping as his lungs filled with fresh air.

"I like rabbit for supper – or I might give it to the dog," Torsa said, "I can't decide. There's so much to eat at home." He smiled sourly, pushing his face into Doran's. "And what will you do about it, boy?" Doran said nothing. Torsa sneered again. "Eat well tonight, then!" he hissed, pushing Doran down over Wolf. "Dog!" he called and Pilot followed him, carefully picking up the rabbits as he passed.

Doran scrambled to his feet. With clenched fists he watched Torsa and Pilot striding away with his dinner.

THREE

Wolf's Return

Doran knelt by the fire. In his hand was a stick with a trout skewered on to the end. Torsa hadn't emptied his trap in the river so at least they had a fish to share. He held it just above the embers as it cooked.

"When will it be ready?" Nico asked, patiently sitting cross-legged next to him.

"Soon."

The fishy smell coiled around the room, filling the two boys with delicious hope. Nico fiddled with Wolf's ears while he waited, his eyes full of the cooking fish. "Can I have some?"

Doran smiled at his little brother and flicked at his arm so they both giggled. "If you must!"

Just then, a dark shape blocked the remaining light from the doorway. The two boys sat rigidly silent but they didn't look round. Their father stood in the gap, a jar of ale in his hand. "What's that dog doin' 'ere? Take it home."

Doran handed half of the cooked fish to Nico, who scuttled off to the back of the hut.

"There's fish," Doran said as he handed the rest of it to his father. Jago took a swig from his jar then belched loudly before taking the fish.

"I'll take the dog back then," Doran said as he stood up. His father grunted. Doran looked around the room, checking that Nico was safely hidden in his deer skin, and then he left.

Wolf padded along behind Doran as they followed the earthen path that wound between the wooden longhouses. Most of the dwellings had stout wooden doors that were shut and barred in the evening. They looked snug and cosy inside. Doran shivered as the warm smell of the forge* drifted on the breeze.

As they rounded the last corner, he could see the red glow of the forge fire reflected in the smooth surface of the metal canopy. The fire was never allowed to go out. Behind it was Rhiannon's home; one of the grandest longhouses of the village. The window shutters were closed now as it was almost dark, but light seeped around the edges. The covered porch spread across the whole length of the building. A storm lantern glimmered brightly next to the central door, causing shadows to dance along the walls.

As soon as Doran reached the outer wall of the forge, a white barn owl flew off the roof and glided silently over their heads into the night. Doran stopped by the outer railing,

16

his fingers resting on Wolf's back. Wisps of smoke hovered above the dark charcoal and an immense heat thawed them both. They could hear the laughter tumbling out from inside of the longhouse but couldn't quite catch what was being said. Wolf let out a low whine.

Without warning the door was flung open, flooding the forge with light from within. Doran shielded his eyes against its brightness.

"It's all right for you," Leon said over his shoulder as he stepped outside, "I've got to go out in the cold and make up the fire for the night."

"Shut the door," Maelbrigte ordered, "you're letting that cold in."

Leon chuckled as he shut the door. Wolf sprang forward, fussing and jumping up at him. "Wolf! Where have you been?" Leon asked in surprise, as he dropped to one knee to hug the dog. Wolf licked Leon's face and wagged his tail. Doran stepped forward then stopped, unsure of his welcome.

"What are you up to?" Leon asked sharply. As he stood up, his right hand instinctively checked for the knife that hung from his belt. Doran shuffled uneasily on the spot and looked down. Leon towered over him, with huge, broad shoulders from working in the forge. Wolf padded to Doran and leaned against his leg. They both looked steadily up at Leon. "You helped the dog?" Leon asked. Doran nodded. "Oh. Well you'd better come in."

Doran sat on the edge of his chair at the head of the table, looking round at Rhiannon's family. At the far end of the room the fire burned brightly and smoke rose up and out through the chimney in the roof. He looked up shyly as he hesitantly explained about how he had looked after Wolf. As he spoke, their faces softened.

"So that's why Leon couldn't find Wolf," Silfor said. "He was in your hut. I guess he didn't think to look there." Silfor looked at Leon, who gave him a sheepish smile. Under the table Wolf lay at Rhiannon's feet, her toes nestling amongst the thick fur of his back. His belly was full of the rabbit that had been waiting for him.

Doran couldn't help looking hungrily at the remains of their food. He could smell the soft tang of the newly baked bread and his stomach grumbled.

"Have you eaten?" Maelbrigte asked. Doran shook his head. His stomach was aching with hunger. "I thought not." Maelbrigte leaned across the table and cut a thick slice from the lamb they'd shared for supper and a big hunk of bread.

"Why didn't you bring Wolf straight here?" Leon asked.

"You were upset about Rhiannon," Doran said through a mouth full of food. "I thought I could help." The lamb melted in his mouth, tasting of the grass in spring. The fire burned brightly, and his face glowed in the warmth of the room.

"I didn't think he could have gone very far. It's not like Wolf to go missing," Leon said. "Besides he always finds his way home, doesn't he Rhiannon?"

A slight shade of pink swept over Rhiannon's face.

"I don't think you can have looked very hard for Wolf, when we sent you out to look for him," Maelbrigte chided her son. She smiled at Doran. "He thinks he's too grown up to be an errand boy any more." Doran returned her smile while he chewed.

"We're very grateful to you," Silfor said solemnly.

Each time Doran swallowed, he winced slightly because of the bruise on his neck. At first he was so hungry he barely noticed it, but with each mouthful it had become more and more painful. He rubbed at the bruise and took another bite. All of them were watching him.

"You look like you've hurt your neck," Maelbrigte said. "How did that happen?"

Doran stopped eating and fiddled with some moss that was stuck to his trousers. He didn't know what to say or how to say it. He wished he was better with words. "Torsa," was all he could think of.

"That boy's a menace," Leon erupted. "He thinks he can push everyone around. He challenged me to a fight last week even though he knows I can beat him. And he waits until you won't notice, Mother, then he starts picking on the little ones." Maelbrigte and Silfor looked at each other across the table. "We need to put him in his place," Leon added fiercely. "Some of the other boys are beginning to look up to him. I don't know if they fear him or respect him. Tell us Doran; why did he hurt you?"

The room fell silent. Doran looked from face to face, his heart beating fast, then he blurted out the tale of how Torsa had stolen his rabbits. When he had finished, Silfor placed his hands on the table and stood up. "I have been talking to Governor Erdig about him," he said. "I know he seems to get away with things, but he comes from a family line of great warriors and one day we might need him. If the Saxons* come this way we'll all have to fight and it won't be pretty. I've heard terrible stories about what they do. We'll need men then who can fight." Silfor's face held a grim expression and no one dared to contradict him.

"I must go home now," Doran said suddenly. "Nico will need me."

Without any further explanation he stuffed the last of the bread in his mouth and stood up to go. Rhiannon walked with him to the door. As she pulled back the wooden bolt to let him out she said, "Thank you for caring for Wolf. Your quick thinking must have saved him." Wolf trotted over and licked Doran's fingers until he smiled and stroked the dog's head gently. "Wolf's grateful, too," she added.

Doran slipped through the door and followed the road back to his hut. He didn't look back, so he didn't know that Rhiannon was watching him go. And he didn't know she'd promised herself she would help him with Torsa.

FOUR

The Prayer to Belisama

All that night Rhiannon tossed about in her sleep. The anger she felt about Torsa had filled her dreams with imagined acts of bravery, but when she woke in the grey, misty morning she knew she wouldn't do any of them. Torsa would always win.

Outside, a light rain turned the dust into a thin smear of mud on the ground, but under the eaves of the forge the drizzle turned to mist by the heat of the fire. Rhiannon dressed to the clanging and hissing from the forge, as Silfor and Leon worked together on an axle for the leatherman's cart.* Once dressed, she dawdled towards the longhouse door to watch them. She loved the smell of the forge, and watching the mysterious transformation that the heat brought to the metal as it was worked.

21

Silfor grasped the long tongs and held the iron bar in the charcoal until it was red hot. Leon worked the bellows,* forcing the air up through the coals. Instantly the charcoal glowed a deep red, crackling with the heat. As soon as the bar developed a white shimmer, Silfor pulled it out onto the retaining wall. Swinging the heavy hammer down onto its hot surface, he hammered it until the bar began to flatten. Leon pumped the bellows again, keeping the coals ready. Sweat covered their faces and dripped onto their stiff leather aprons. Rhiannon stepped back behind the door with a start as she noticed Torsa standing in the rain, watching the men at work. His hair was a sodden mass, but he didn't seem to care.

"Why does it need all that hammering?" Torsa asked.

Silfor looked up at him. "It gives the iron strength. May Gobannus* be praised! He takes the strength from a man's arm and gives it to the iron. Without it the bar would break as soon as the cart hit the first rut in the road; a wooden axle is better than unworked iron."

"So is that what gives a sword its power?"

Silfor winked across at Leon. "Well that depends; the metal needs to be worked but mixing in other things helps, too."

Torsa came closer so he could see the iron more clearly. "Do you have what you'd need to make me a sword?"

Silfor raised his eyebrows at Leon. "Possibly. Have you earned the right to have one?"

"No. But I will. Soon."

Leon stopped pumping the bellows and the two men watched Torsa saunter away, his great black hound at his heels as ever. "He'll be more dangerous than ever with a sword," Leon said to his father.

"Peace, Leon. If the boy is to fight for us then we need to arm him well."

"Will Gobannus preserve him?"

"I think that boy is looking for more danger than even Gobannus could protect a man from." Leon nodded in agreement, as he put on his leather gauntlets* and lifted up the crucible of molten metal with huge tongs. It had been nestling in the red-hot charcoal towards the back of the fire. Carefully, he poured it into the shaped mould. The molten metal cracked and spat as it cooled.

Rhiannon watched Torsa walk away. His rain-soaked hair rested on his thick torc like seaweed on a rock. *He wants to be a warrior as his father was before him, but really he likes nothing better than hurting others*, she thought. She pulled out her knife from its sheath and laid it across the palm of her hand, thinking of the day she made it with her father. Suddenly she had an idea. She pulled herself a little taller and slipped the knife back in its sheath. *If Gobannus protected those who work with metal, perhaps Belisama would protect Doran if she asked her!* Ever since she had been a little girl her father had told her the same story, of how the Roman god Belisama had stayed in the river when the army left. In times of peril the Brigantes had called on her for aid. If you wanted her help you had to write a prayer on lead, the way the Romans had, then drop it into the river.

Rhiannon walked over to the forge. An idea was blossoming in her mind. Now the iron had been worked, Leon and Silfor had gone to sort through the broken scrap,* so she was alone. She searched amongst the piles of discarded pieces until she found what she was looking for. Underneath all the off-cuts was a small square of bendy lead about the size of her palm. She held it up to the light and smiled; it was perfect.

I'll make a prayer for Doran, and drop it in the river, she decided. Belisama would surely protect him from Torsa, just as she had helped her father, and his fathers before that. She picked up the long thin scratch-awl* from the bench, and put it with the lead into the pocket that hung from her belt.

"Come, Wolf," she ordered, as she walked back to pick up her pike from behind the longhouse door. "I'm going fishing," she called out as she left the house. She and Wolf walked together through the village and out through the great gates. She smiled with pride as she thought about the good she would do with her prayer.

The finches were chattering in the budding trees when they walked down the slope, as if they, too, were discussing her errand. The rain had stopped and Wolf trotted on ahead, sniffing at the wet grass and amongst the bushes; his tail twitching contentedly. Every now and then he stopped and looked up for her, wagging his tail until she caught him up, before trotting off ahead again. Rhiannon loved her dog and her heart was full of gratitude that Doran had helped him. Now she was going to help Doran in return; he had always been a good friend.

When she arrived at the river, Rhiannon stood on the

24

bank looking at the cold, grey water. She shivered as she thought about the black crow and the water smothering her. How had she got out of the river? Her memories were all jumbled. Hadn't someone pulled her out? She shook that thought from her head and settled comfortably on a flat rock on the bank, just down from the stepping stones. It was better not to think about that. The sun now shone, sparkling on the rippling water's surface and a heron stood motionless, staring at the fish that moved around his toes. It all looked so different now.

Wolf lay at Rhiannon's feet, with his head on his paws. "What shall we put as our prayer?" she asked him. "Belisama is great and powerful, the protector of men and gatherer of souls. We could start with that black crow." Wolf's ears twitched in approval.

Rhiannon worked the picture slowly. Her tongue stuck out from between her lips as she marked the metal with the scratching awl. Each time she turned the lead she absent-mindedly caught Wolf with her foot, but he didn't seem to mind. "What shall we put next? We need to ask for protection for Doran from the cruelty of Torsa, so maybe we need to draw them." Rhiannon sucked the end of the awl as she looked over the river deep in thought. "I'll draw Torsa in a tree waiting to ambush Doran while he's fishing." Her eyes met the dog's and she smiled before putting her scratching awl to work once more.

When she had finished, she drew leaves all around the edge, with peeping eyes amongst the leaves, just like the enamel brooch her mother wore. "There!" She leaned back, admiring her handiwork. "That would please anyone!" She stood and looked up and down the river. "Now, Wolf, where shall we drop it?"

In the quiet shallows by the long bend she saw a flash of emerald as a kingfisher dropped into the water after fish. But when she looked back Wolf was standing by the stepping stones. Rhiannon looked at him and considered. "You're right. There'll be no gain if there's no danger."

But when she stood looking at the first stone her mouth felt dry. The river swirled noisily around it, pushing and shoving. The muscles of her back clamped in a chain of fear as the cold grey water coiled into white foaming snakes. She licked her dry lips, looked up into Wolf's eyes, took in a deep breath and made up her mind to move. Like an emperor walking out onto the battlefield she strode across the stones to the centre of the river.

"Hail! O mighty Belisama," she called aloud, "I present to you my prayer and ask for your aid for my friend." With that she dropped the lead prayer into the water, where it was caught by the current and whisked away.

Later that morning Rhiannon walked back up the slow rise towards the great gates, humming quietly to herself. Four fat trout were hanging from the end of the fishing pike she held over her shoulder. She had caught them in the quiet shallows by the long bend. Great clouds like floating mountains sailed above her, threatening to pour their rain back upon the earth. She shivered and let the fingers of her free hand rest amongst the fur of Wolf's back as they walked along together.

She felt Wolf stiffen as Pilot appeared suddenly from the

edge of the woodland, trotting fearlessly towards the gates, followed by Torsa. He carried three rabbits by their tails, carelessly tossed over his right shoulder, and was smiling to himself.

"Where has he got those rabbits from?" Rhiannon wondered, frowning. "He's too busy practising his fighting to set traps. I hope he's not taken Doran's rabbits again!"

Rhiannon's chest heaved with a sudden burst of anger and she clenched her fists. She needed Belisama to answer her prayer as quickly as possible.

FIVE

The Training Battle

Torsa's eyes were narrowed slits. His tongue slipped between pursed lips as he took aim. The handle of the longbow* was in his left hand, with his arm outstretched towards the target. His right elbow was pulled back behind his shoulder so that the string was rigidly taught; the feathers of his arrow quivered with the strain. A gentle breeze ruffled his hair as the whole group of children waited for him to fire.

Rhiannon stretched onto the tips of her toes so she could see over the tops of the boys' heads. *Torsa will be unbearable if he makes this*, she thought. No child had ever managed to hit the target from this distance – not since her mother had trained.

Miriam nudged her. "What do you think?" she whispered.

"He'll never make it, surely. He'll be insufferable if he does."

All eyes were on Torsa. No one spoke. Every nerve was strained like the bow. Every breath caught as the string twanged and the arrow thrummed its way across the field. A collective sigh filled the air as it flew straight into the heart of the straw man that was propped against the farthest tree.

"Well done," Maelbrigte said, her voice rich with respect.

Rhiannon slowly shook her head in disbelief. Now Torsa's head would be swollen even more. All the children started talking at once; trying to judge the distance, slapping Torsa on the back and hugging each other. Rhiannon and Miriam allowed themselves to be jostled to the back of the group and sat together on a boulder at the edge of the clearing.

"Goodness," Miriam whispered. "I didn't think he'd really do it, did you?"

Rhiannon shook her head gloomily. "They're all going to love him now."

Torsa stood surrounded by the other boys and girls like a jewel in a crown. His back was straight and his chest proud. He was smiling but his eyes were cold, like a snake's.

Maelbrigte walked over to him and everyone fell silent. "I think you might be ready to start your training with the men," she declared.

"So Torsa will learn how to use the training sword* then," Miriam whispered to Rhiannon, "if he's going to start training with the men."

Maelbrigte silenced the group with a look. "This afternoon we will go back to the main yard and let Torsa show his skill to the elders, to see if he's ready to train with the adults. We'll practise fighting in a circle so they can watch him more easily. Remember, you need to know who is at your back. While you're concentrating on one opponent, anyone can get behind you and take you by surprise. Torsa, you must take on all the other children but I'll give you two others to form a circle with. Let's show everyone how much you have all learned!"

Maelbrigte scanned their eager faces. Rhiannon and Miriam shared an expectant look. "Rhiannon and Miriam, you'll stand with Torsa and take on the rest. Torsa; I think you're ready to have a try with the training sword when we get back. You may take it from the wall for a while."

For a moment the group was stunned. Smiling, Torsa made a slight bow in agreement, but sneered behind her back.

Rhiannon shuddered at the look on his face. He was so pleased with himself, but he had no respect for her mother.

"Don't forget your pikes for the battle," Maelbrigte reminded the children, who groaned in unison.

Later that day, the children began to collect in the main yard. "Keep close to me," Rhiannon said to Miriam. "Torsa won't help us so we need to stick together."

They walked across the hard, baked earth towards Torsa. He stood before the Governor's longhouse, holding the training sword in his right hand with the blade resting across his left palm. He turned it slightly so the sun caught in the inscription along its blade as he read it.

"Do you know what it says?" Miriam asked.

"*May strength prevail*. My father says the Roman army left it behind."

"Have you ever had a go with it?"

"Not exactly. I've held it when my father took it home to sharpen it. It's very heavy."

"Well, I hope it will always be too heavy for me," Miriam said, chuckling at the thought. "I don't ever want to fight in real life."

They stood side by side as they watched Torsa hoist the blade towards the sun and then swing it down in great arcs either side of him. If he did well in training, he would get his own sword. He looked impressive as he controlled the blade. Pilot padded across to him. He made a wide circle around his master, then dropped down onto the floor with his muzzle on his paws.

Silfor and Leon came round the corner of the main street. Rhiannon waved her pike in the air and they waved back. They stepped onto the porch of Governor Erdig's longhouse and sat with the other other men who had already taken their seats. Maelbrigte sat on the farthest edge, watching Torsa. Wolf padded across and leaned against Leon's leg. He patted his head and smiled across the yard at Rhiannon, warming her heart. "Let's show them our skills, as well," Rhiannon said, and Miriam nodded.

Governor Erdig came out of the door of his longhouse. He was old, but he was still tall and straight. His skin was weathered to the colour of acorns and his thin grey

31

hair was neatly tied in a ponytail. He wore a large circular pin at his chest, enamelled with green leaves. It held his leather cloak, which was pushed back over both shoulders. Rhiannon watched as he quietly chatted with her mother before taking his seat at the centre.

"It's time to return the sword," Erdig called to Torsa, "so we can begin."

Torsa exchanged the sword for his pike and walked across the yard towards the girls. "Protect my back," he ordered, before turning away.

Miriam's eyebrows shot up as she looked across at Rhiannon who made a small mock bow as she turned. The three stood with their backs to each other and their pikes raised across their chests in readiness for the onslaught. Rhiannon's heart beat soundly in her chest as she steadied herself.

Slowly, parents began to gather round the edges of the yard to watch the training battle. Maelbrigte stood up and the crowd fell silent, waiting for her to speak. "We're here to assess Torsa. To see if he can move to work with the men. He must be valiant against all the children and I've selected Miriam and Rhiannon to fight with him. Afterwards we will talk about his skill and make a decision together." She raised her hand. "Let the battle begin!"

Rhiannon heard the pounding of small feet thundering on the hard earth; then the gaggle of settlement children surged around the corner into the main yard. "Here they come," she whispered. With their pikes held high, the children charged towards the three of them. Miriam's pike trembled slightly so the pack headed straight for her.

32

"Steady," Rhiannon said. But Torsa pushed the girls aside so he could face the charging children himself. He let out a huge roar – and then knocked down the first three boys with a mighty swing of his pike.

"Good attack, Torsa!" Maelbrigte called from the porch.

The rest of the pack fanned out around the circle. Rhiannon bent forward, spreading out her arms to fill the gaps between herself and the others. Miriam followed her example. Torsa saw his chance and thrust the butt of his pike into the chest of the tallest girl, winding her and sending her over.

Rhiannon growled fiercely at three small girls, showing her teeth like an angry dog. They all ran for safety, screaming and crying. A low chuckle ran through the parents. Now there were just five strong boys left in the pack.

"Come on then," Torsa goaded them, shaking his pike. Rhiannon took her chance and charged at the red headed twins, chasing them back across the yard, forgetting to keep the circle strong. Two of the older boys rushed through the gap she'd made, grabbed Miriam and dragged her face down in the dirt.

Rhiannon sped across the yard after the twins. Behind her Torsa was invincible. He chopped the legs from under the first boy with a swing of his pike, bringing him face down on the ground. Then he brought it straight back, elbowing one of Miriam's assailants in the midriff, knocking him to the floor. Then, he parried the thrust of a third boy, shattering his pike.

At the far side of the yard the twins skidded to a stop and faced Rhiannon; spreading themselves apart so she had to choose which one to face. She was caught like a rat in a trap, twisting back and forth to parry the thrusts of the twins as they took turns in stabbing at her.

Torsa howled like a wild boar. As he charged across the yard towards her, Rhiannon could see the blood lust in his eyes. He slapped one twin across the back, knocking him into Rhiannon so their heads crashed together. They crumpled over one another as they fell to the ground in a groggy heap. Then the second twin landed on top of them, his face hanging in front of Rhiannon's. She could see the bruise beginning to form on his cheek as he slid to the ground.

"Enough!" Maelbrigte called as she ran towards them.

Rhiannon sat on the ground, looking up at Torsa, who thrust his pike up to the sky, threw back his head and crowed like a cockerel.

Rhiannon's head pounded and tiny silver dots swam before her eyes. She sat between the twins, breathing hard. Wolf trotted over and licked her face. "I'm all right," she snapped, pushing him away.

As her vision cleared she saw Doran walk through the gate on the other side of the yard, his hoe balanced over his right shoulder. When he saw her on the ground he started to run towards her. She smiled at him, but Torsa charged across the yard and grabbed his tunic. He lifted Doran right up onto his toes and spat in his face.

Rhiannon tried to get up, but her legs were weak and shaky. She watched her mother take Torsa and Doran by the arm and lead them over to Governor Erdig's porch.

"He'll pay," she heard Torsa shout, as he waved his fist at Doran. He pulled away from Maelbrigte and swaggered away, followed by a gaggle of younger boys like a tail to a comet.

When it was time to go home, Rhiannon followed her family down the lane, but suddenly stopped. "I've left my cloak in the yard," she remembered.

"You'd better go and fetch it then," Silfor replied. "Wolf! Heel!" he ordered. Wolf trotted obediently behind him.

The yard was empty and quiet as Rhiannon entered it from the main street. The sun was low in the sky, turning it amber above the fence line. Rhiannon screwed up her eyes against its glare. She soon found her cloak, but as she picked it up she heard a faint squeal, like a dog trapped by its paw. She looked back over towards the main group of longhouses but couldn't see anything. As she started to walk back she heard the squeal again. It sounded like something in pain. She listened. A low piercing cry came from behind the first longhouse. Rhiannon walked cautiously towards it.

The ginnel* was blocked by Pilot, his feet planted squarely and his head low. He watched her, menacingly. Rhiannon licked her dry lips. *I wish Wolf was here*, she thought. Pilot growled at her, his white fangs clearly visible. Behind him was Torsa, who appeared to be holding up something – or somebody.

"Tomorrow, you snivelling wretch," she heard him say, "we'll see how brave you are."

35

"Torsa?" she called. "What's going on?" Pilot growled and edged towards her.

There was a muffled thud as Torsa turned and walked away down the ginnel. "Come," he said to the dog, without looking at Rhiannon. Pilot turned and followed him. It was only then that Rhiannon could see the crumpled form of Doran in a heap on the ground.

"What's happening?" she asked, rushing down the ginnel and kneeling beside him. His grimy face was streaked with blood. "What's he done?"

Doran tried to smile, wincing with pain. "It's my own fault, I spat back at him." He shook his head sadly. "Now I will have to fight."

Rhiannon frowned. "What do you mean, fight?"

"Tomorrow at the hunt."

She shook her head in irritation. "What do you mean?"

Doran looked at her and sighed. "You can't help me, Rhiannon. Just leave me alone."

SIX

Thinking Things Over

The eerie hoot of the owl tore at the silence as Rhiannon sat on the bottom step of the stairs to the loft where she slept. She smiled. The good omen the owl brought filled her with a strong sense of safety, but still her heart was heavy with worries. She wanted to talk to her parents about Torsa and Doran, but it was late. Her head rested on the thin wall which separated her parents' bedroom from the rest of the house. The planks were roughly put together, which meant she could peek into the room through the cracks.

Her mother lay back against the soft pillow that was stuffed with sheep's wool, her head resting against the outer wall. Maelbrigte was watching Silfor washing in the bowl, stripped to the waist. It was a ritual he undertook every

37

evening. The delicate smell of rose water drifted through the planks as she watched them.

"Are we ready for the boar hunt in the morning?" Maelbrigte asked. "It's been a busy day and I've not thought much about it."

"Hmm," he muttered in assent, his face still dripping over the bowl. Rhiannon could only see the back of his head as he brought up the cloth to dry his face. "We all know what to do. Governor Erdig is sure where most of the boar are this season."

Maelbrigte nodded. "Good. It isn't right that Doran missed the training again, though. He'd make a fine warrior. He just needs more practice."

"I've been thinking of trying him with the men tomorrow," Silfor said as he dried his hands. "He's good with that pike even if he misses your practices."

Maelbrigte nodded but her doubts showed clearly on her face. Rhiannon was surprised. Doran, with the men?

"Now look," Silfor responded, as he climbed into bed alongside his wife. "It's only a boar hunt, not a proper battle. If Doran didn't work so hard they would all starve. As it is he can scarcely find enough food. He wasn't romping round the woodlands enjoying himself, he was planting for next year."

"I know," Maelbrigte winced. "I know he needs our help, not our pity. But are you sure he'll be safe with the men?"

Rhiannon pushed open the door and stood in the entrance to the bedroom. Both her parents looked at her in surprise. "Shouldn't you be in bed asleep?" Maelbrigte asked. Rhiannon's words of reply dried up in her mouth.

"Come," Silfor said, and Rhiannon climbed into the bed next to him.

"I'm worried that Torsa will hurt Doran," she said.

Silfor looked at her. "Why?"

Rhiannon sighed. "I'm not sure; it's something to do with today's fight."

"You were careless today," Maelbrigte complained. "I don't know what got into you." Rhiannon's face tinged with pink and she looked down at her hands. "You let Miriam down when you left the circle. In a real fight she could have been killed. You should have kept the circle strong."

"I thought I could get the twins," Rhiannon replied defiantly, but she knew in her heart her mother was right.

"Torsa was magnificent. He took them all out single-handedly," Silfor said. "He made up for your mistake." They all sat in silence for a while, then Maelbrigte said, "You don't work well with Torsa, do you? You don't like or trust him and that changes how you act."

Rhiannon nodded. It was true.

Silfor ran his fingers through his greying hair and loosened it from its pony tail. It fell around his face, making him look instantly older. "Torsa doesn't work in a team and that affects them all." He rested his head back against the pillow. "I think the others are afraid of him."

After a while Maelbrigte added, "You know, you're right. They look for his approval or his rejection. It hampers them."

Silfor put his arm around Rhiannon's shoulder and hugged her. "I'm always proud of how you fight; you're fearless like your mother." Rhiannon sighed, the weight of worry lifting a little from her.

"Torsa was ready for the sword," Maelbrigte said. "His longbow was almost as good as mine."

"I'd heard it was better!" Silfor said, giving Rhiannon a conspiratorial hug.

Maelbrigte looked at them both in mock horror. "Never!" she said, laughing.

"Now off you go to bed," Silfor said, gently pushing Rhiannon away. "And don't worry."

"You need to keep an eye on Doran tomorrow," she heard Maelbrigte say to her father as she walked to the door. She glanced back at them as she closed it, but Silfor was already drifting off to sleep.

Rhiannon climbed the steep stairs up to the loft and clambered into the deer skin on her wooden bed. Wolf was curled up at the end waiting for her, so she pushed her feet beneath him. He settled himself again and his eyes closed, but Rhiannon couldn't sleep. Her thoughts whirled round and round. "Surely Belisama should have made a difference by now?" she whispered in the silence. "Was she not listening to me? Should I have written something better in the prayer? Have I praised her enough?"

Rhiannon rolled over onto her other side, moving her feet under Wolf's flank. "How do you get these gods to explain? It's such a tricky business."

Suddenly Rhiannon sat up, dragging her feet from under Wolf. "It's not fair! I keep trying and trying to make a difference and Belisama does nothing. How do I get her to help? It's all too distant, like catching butterflies in the breeze. I've no idea if I'm doing the right thing or not. I could be making it worse, Wolf!"

Wolf sat up, stretched back on his haunches and yawned. He looked quizzically at Rhiannon. "It's no good looking like that," she hissed. "I can't sleep." Wolf lay his head back on his paws. "We need to stay near Doran tomorrow. You need to keep Pilot at bay." Wolf's tail made a feeble wag. "Tomorrow you stick with Doran. He could use a good dog if he's hunting with the men. He will need protection." Wolf blinked at her.

"I'll be all right," she said, in answer to his unasked question. "I can take care of myself. I can climb a tree at the first sight of trouble. And I've got my knife." Wolf sighed. "You never know – Belisama might just make things better." Wolf yawned and Rhiannon laid down again. "We need to be brave tomorrow, Wolf. It's going to be a big day."

SEVEN

The Boar Hunt

The sun streaked the sky red as dawn broke. Most of the villagers were already assembling in the main yard for the biannual boar hunt. At least one person from every family went to hunt, so they could have their share of the meat and leather when the hunt was over. Mainly it was the men who went, but some of the women and girls went, too. They stood in family groups; checking they had all they needed. Some of the men were testing the strength of their pikes or bow strings.

Miriam walked through the crowd with a jar of water. "Have you got enough water?" she asked everyone as she passed. Every now and then she'd top up a flask, teasing the young men about their strength. Excitement ran through

42

the group like wind through the trees. Everyone was smiling and helping each other, chatting about previous hunts and the meat feast they'd be bringing home.

Doran slunk around the edge of the large group, scowling. He carried his pike in his right hand. Nico sidled up behind him, his hand searching for the strong grip of his older brother. Doran didn't look down, but a stray smile flickered on his lips. "What d'you want?" he asked.

Nico's thumb absently slipped into his mouth. "Nothin'."

"Give over," Doran hissed as he pushed the thumb out. "What will Dad say if he sees you with your thumb in your mouth?" Nico's eyes filled with tears as he leaned against his older brother.

"I'll be all right," Doran gently promised. Nico nodded, unsure. "There's nothing to be afraid of. Dad's asleep at home, but you can stay with Miriam and her little brothers. She said she'd look after you while I'm hunting."

"What if they get you?" Nico asked.

"That's not very likely, is it? I can run fast and my pike is sharp. I'll not be trapped by a pig," Doran assured him, "and then we can have our share of the roast." The two boys laughed together at that hungry thought. "Be off." Doran pushed Nico towards Miriam who held out her hand for him, smiling.

As Nico left Doran's side, Wolf replaced him. He sat on his haunches neatly under Doran's hand. Doran smiled at him in surprise. "Hello boy. What are you doing here?" Wolf looked up at him and his tail wagged across the earth behind him. Doran looked over to where Rhiannon stood near him, with her father and Leon. He heard Leon ask his sister where Wolf was.

"He's over there. I'm not worrying about him today. He doesn't always have to be with me."

"Is that wise?" Leon said.

Rhiannon looked up at the sky. "He'll slow me down watching out for him."

"That doesn't sound like Wolf to me. I'd have thought he'd be watching out for *you*."

Rhiannon smiled weakly at her brother. Doran stroked Wolf's head and strolled over to stand next to her. Wolf's eyes locked on Pilot's as he padded towards them, following Torsa. Doran followed his gaze and shuddered. The fur on the back of Wolf's neck stood up and a low growl rumbled within him. "Easy," Doran said, "let's not provoke them." He stroked Wolf's head gently, as Torsa and Pilot walked proudly past.

Governor Erdig stood on the top step of his longhouse. "Gather round!" he called in a loud voice. The eager crowd jostled around him. "Today we run through the North Woods," he said, "then out to the great plain. It's a fair walk, but there are plenty of boar in the woods and we will kill them as they come out of the cover. Maelbrigte will lead the archers to make a stand as the pigs come out of the wood onto the plain. May the gods bless our run today and fill our larders with plenty. Let the hunt begin!"

Maelbrigte nodded and started to walk towards the gate. "Archers, let's go!" The other archers followed her, testing the tightness of their bow strings as they walked.

"Torsa," Erdig continued, "I want you to run with the archers today. Maelbrigte has told me about your shooting yesterday, so you're ready."

"Well done," one of the men said amiably to Torsa as they fell in step together behind Maelbrigte. But Torsa didn't look pleased. He walked away, his head proud.

As Torsa left, Doran felt a wave of relief wash through him. Torsa couldn't find him to hurt him if he was with the archers. Doran looked at Rhiannon and she rolled her eyes, making him smile. It would be a good day, after all. As he watched the archers marching down the hill towards the woods, lost in thought, he noticed one of the other archers handing Torsa a bow. Torsa snatched it grumpily and then walked on without a word. *He can't even say thanks*, Doran thought.

"Doran and Rhiannon," Governor Erdig said, making him jump, "Silfor tells me you are both ready to help the men flush out the boar."

Doran stared up at Governor Erdig; he couldn't quite believe he had such an important role in the hunt. But when he glanced at Rhiannon she looked tall and proud and prepared, so he nodded and smiled.

Doran watched with the others as they waited for the archers to pass the allotments and reach the path that led towards the North Wood. The broad valley lay expectantly before them with the woods steaming in the early morning sunshine. He was always comforted by this view from the gate. Surely today would be a good day?

Silfor touched his arm lightly. "I've been warning Rhiannon," he said, "don't go out of the north side of the wood or you'll run into the archers. They'll not expect you coming and might mistake you for a boar."

Doran nodded. "I'll be careful."

Rhiannon smiled at him as she drew her knife out of its scabbard. She turned the blade in the light. Doran could see the long snakes with many eyes her father had etched upon its blade, to help her see all around in a fight. That morning her mother had plaited her hair into two long, snaking lengths from her temple down each side of her head. *They care so much for her*, he thought, as a familiar trickle of sadness ran through his body.

Nico's small hand slipped into his own again. "Now what?" Doran said, impatiently.

"Be careful."

Doran smiled at his little brother. "I'll be fine." He waited while Miriam took hold of Nico's hand and led him away with the other children. She, too, rolled her eyes at him. Suddenly, Doran realised that his childhood had left him. Now he was a man, and had to act like one.

"Let's go!" Governor Erdig called and all the remaining hunters started down the slope after him. Doran followed Silfor, Leon and Rhiannon. A gaggle of working dogs from the settlement jostled along around them, ready to help with the hunt.

When they finally reached the North Wood, the hunters spread out along its border, each taking a wide swathe of woodland to work through. The plan was, as always, to force the boar to run forwards and out to the plain. Doran found himself at the furthest edge. He quietened his footsteps as he moved onward, listening. He heard the pigs before he saw them, and smiled. There was his meat! He paused, listening, then sprang forward to startle them, but instead of running away towards the plain, the pack began to run in all directions. Doran's heart beat faster and he steadied himself, unable to let the chance of a strike go. Holding his pike high by his shoulder, his eyes locked on to the back of a medium-sized speckled boar. All his concentration was on the strike he shouldn't really make.

Suddenly a huge weight hit him between the shoulders, forcing all the air from his lungs. Doran fell forward, his pike flying lamely ahead of him. He fell on his knees but the weight kept pushing him forward until his face was in the dirt. Panic clutched his heart like a vice. Slobber drooled round his chin. *Pilot*! Sharp teeth fastened around his neck like a great clamp. Doran's feet scrabbled against the earth, trying to get purchase to push himself up, but Pilot's body spread on top of him, forcing him down, grinding his face into the earth, dragging it from side to side. Mud filled his mouth and gravel scraped his skin. He couldn't get his breath. He scrabbled his hands in the dirt in desperation. His ears filled with a buzzing noise. He began to go limp.

Then a huge surge of cool clean air filled his lungs as Pilot was thrown off his body and landed with a crash next to him, slewing across the bracken. Wolf was clinging to Pilot's back, his teeth ripping into one of his ears.

Gasping for breath, Doran watched Pilot and Wolf roll over and over away from him, biting and snarling at each other. Fur and blood spattered the undergrowth as they fought in fury, churning the ground into mud. Wolf's back paws ripped at Pilot's underbelly as they rolled, but Pilot had gripped Wolf's neck like a vice, desperately trying to snap it. Over and over they rolled, away from Doran.

Shakily, Doran got to his feet. He stood there, swaying, then he turned and ran back towards where he thought the others would be. On and on he ran, the blood from the wound on his neck turning his shredded tunic a sticky red. He stumbled over the clumps of grass that seemed to obstruct his way. He lost all sense of direction as he crashed back and forth in the undergrowth, the twigs and brambles tearing at him as he ran. Then suddenly he crashed through the trees into the open plain. He skidded to a stop, panting, his hands on his knees as he caught his breath.

Slowly, he raised his head and looked across the vast expanse of grass. In the distance he saw Torsa smile in delight, raise his longbow and release an arrow directly at him. Doran glimpsed the spinning arrow as it came towards him, just before his body hit the ground.

EIGHT

Cornered

Deep in the wood Silfor and Rhiannon were following boar tracks through the bracken.

"I think we've lost this one," Silfor said over his shoulder. "I think it must have cut back to the pack." Suddenly her father stopped. "That sounds like dogs fighting," he said. His head turned slightly so he could catch the noise. "Over there, I think." He pointed the way with his pike. Rhiannon stopped, too. She hoped Wolf was with Doran. They both listened, but Rhiannon could hear nothing except the wind in the trees.

Silfor headed in the direction of the noise. Rhiannon followed closely on her father's heels. The damp, acrid smell of the broken bracken was oppressive, but she knew better than to complain or talk. She, too, listened intently, as a boar could come at any time or from any direction. Then on the breeze she thought she could hear the faint sound of a dog whining. "Did you hear that?" she whispered.

Her father stood listening but could hear only the creaks and groaning sounds of the wood. He shook his head. They walked on. They did not see Wolf lying on the ground, his eyes closed, ears torn and breathing laboured, or the hoof marks of the boar that had trampled him, freeing him from Pilot's hold.

They paused in a clearing. "Nothing," Silfor said at last.

"Perhaps we were mistaken," Rhiannon replied.

"I'm sure I heard something." Silfor sat on a fallen trunk and took out a flask of water from his pocket. He held it up for her. The water was warm on the back of her throat. "Did you see Pilot a few minutes ago?" he asked. "He looked like he was stalking something."

Rhiannon shook her head. "No."

"I might be mistaken, but he looked like he was trailing Doran." Rhiannon stared at her father wide-eyed, but before she could speak he was on his feet. "Quick, this way!" he said.

Silfor was off again, but this time they could both hear the snorting of a pig. He began to run in great, even strides, his pike in his right hand. Rhiannon had trouble keeping up with him. Way ahead of her he jumped over a fallen trunk and then disappeared into a thicket. As she pushed through the undergrowth after him she saw he had cornered a large sow, who was standing her ground against the bent root of a tree. Her massive body tried to hide the piglets that she was ready to die to protect. The piglets lay silently under the root, listening. She barked in anger as Silfor and Rhiannon edged slowly towards her. Rhiannon had her knife out but Silfor raised his pike to his shoulder in readiness to strike. "She's a beauty," he said, keeping his eyes fixed on the prize. "Go round the other side, Rhiannon."

Rhiannon slowly made her way to the opposite side of the pig, who barked again. "She sounds very angry," Rhiannon said, feeling unsure.

A loud crash of splintering wood echoed from behind the tree, making them both turn. "Go, Rhiannon!" shouted Silfor, as he turned to face the oncoming hog; his pike poised to strike. "Run!" The enormous male boar sped round the trunk, its back feet scrabbling in the dirt with the speed of its turn. For a moment, Rhiannon froze in terror. Then she turned on her heels and fled, knife in hand.

Behind her she could hear the piercing squeal as Silfor's pike struck the boar. Her pace slowed and she smiled. Her father had got the hog! Intending to go back, she stopped and put her knife back in its sheath. But as she turned, she saw the sow running through the undergrowth towards her.

Rhiannon ran away in terror. The huge, angry sow was at her heels, snapping each time she got close enough. After a while Rhiannon's chest heaved, but she couldn't stop. Down the bank towards the grassy plain she slithered as fast as she could, with the sow snarling behind her. Then she saw a hazel tree with a sturdy low branch. She made a sudden leap and swung herself into it. She quickly pulled up her legs before climbing up onto the next branch.

The sow snarled and snapped around the base of the

tree. Rhiannon clung to the trunk, getting her breath back, looking down into angry eyes. The sow butted and dug at the base of the tree, shaking it with all her strength, but slowly the rattling of the tree eased and Rhiannon's pounding heart slowed.

"Go away!" she yelled down at the pig, but the sow still paced round the tree. Rhiannon's stomach grumbled, reminding her that breakfast had been a long time ago. *I wish I had something to eat*, she thought. Rhiannon looked about her but there was nothing to hand. She dared not leave the safety of the tree, so she climbed a little higher. A small pool of water had collected in the crook of a branch and she gulped it, thirstily.

When she looked up she saw a bunch of hazel nuts clustered together that had been left hanging there all winter. Rhiannon climbed up to collect the bounty, then sat astride a sturdy branch with her back to the trunk to eat. "Now what do I do?" she asked herself, looking down. The pig was still there. She looked about the canopy of trees but had no idea where she was, or where everyone else was – or which way was home. She swivelled round to look behind her. *That shiny snake must be the river*, she thought. *If I go in that direction and find it, I'll be able to find my way home, even if I don't find the others.* She made herself comfortable and told herself she would just have to wait until it was safe to go.

She must have dropped off. When she woke, the sun was dropping behind the trees. Rhiannon couldn't see the base of the tree through the branches, but all had gone quiet. She dropped a nutshell to test if the pig was still waiting. Nothing. She climbed down to the lowest branch and looked all round. The sow had gone. Slowly she lowered herself to the woodland floor. "I'm sure the river was this way," she said aloud, as if to bolster her own confidence. "I'll soon find it and follow it home."

But down in the dark of the wood, things looked quite different. As she trudged along, she wished with all her heart she had Wolf by her side.

NINE

Lost in the Darkness

It wasn't until the blisters began to burn her feet that Rhiannon admitted to herself that she was completely lost. How could she have she missed the river, when it had looked so clear from the tree? She plonked herself down on a fallen tree trunk and cupped her chin in her hands.

"What am I going to do now?" she whispered to herself. Tears filled her eyes. Her feet hurt, her arms ached from the tree climb, the sun was going down and she was lost. And there was no Wolf to comfort her.

Tears won't get me home, she thought. Her stomach grumbled, reminding her that she'd only eaten nuts since breakfast. "What would father do?" she asked herself aloud.

Rhiannon, don't ever let the panic take you. Think and plan, Silfor said from her memory. *Get up and act. Don't sit there feeling sorry for yourself. You have to act to survive.*

She wiped her nose on her sleeve, rubbed the tears from her eyes, and looked around her. To one side was a tall conifer. "If I climb that I can see where I am," she decided.

Although weariness was soaking into her bones like water on sand, she pulled herself onto the lowest branch and looked up the trunk. The rough branches grew out evenly, so she could climb it like a ladder. It was hard work, but as she neared the top, the branches were more spaced out, which meant she could see over the canopy of the wood. The land opened up beneath her like a map. To her right was the river, just a few trees away, but her heart sank as she realised the settlement must still be a long way off.

The sun was a great red ball moving towards the horizon, like a dragon waiting in ambush. "It's starting to get dark," she whispered to herself. "If I'm not quick, I'm not going to get back before the gates shut and Wolf isn't here to protect me." The thought settled uncomfortably in the pit of her stomach. There was no point in praying to Belisama now evening was on its way, yet the desire for help overwhelmed her.

As she gazed a little upstream, she saw what looked like a coracle* beached on the shingle. She strained her eyes to see through the gloom of the overhanging trees. Was it a boat? A short distance inland she saw a thin wisp of smoke. *Perhaps someone can help me*, she thought. Once again, the vague memory of someone pulling her from the water came back to her.

55

Rhiannon clambered down the tree, but when she started to walk, the blisters tore at her heels, making her limp. A great hand of fear clutched her stomach, squeezing out her strength. *What if the boat belongs to one of those marauding gangs father talks of sometimes?* she fretted.

But still she walked on through the trees and finally she saw the river. When she reached the bank, she saw the glow of a small fire. *That can't be a great gang,* she thought, peering round a tree. *Perhaps it's a family, travelling.* She stood for a moment, considering her options, wishing Wolf was with her.

As she crept closer, Rhiannon made out the shape of a man bending over a small heap of sticks. He looked odd – unlike anyone she'd met before. He wore a dark cloak that was crumpled round his heels and the top of his head was shaved in a small circle. He was humming to himself as he stirred something in a pot on the fire. She paused, watching him – and she thought again about the person who had rescued her from the river.

"Do you need help?" the man asked. His accent was strange and unfamiliar, but his voice was clear and strong.

"Yes," Rhiannon whispered, the pulse in her temple twitching.

The man stood up and turned around. "Hungry?"

Rhiannon stared. Whatever she was expecting, it wasn't this. The man was clearly young. He had a neatly trimmed beard which covered most of his face and the kindest brown eyes Rhiannon had ever seen. But the most surprising thing of all was that he wore no leather belt with a knife or sword hanging from it. He was wearing a simple brown garment under his cloak, with a knotted rope around his waist.* He had no enamelled brooch to fasten his cloak, nor did he wear a torc. There was just a wooden cross hanging round his neck on a string. "You're not Brigantes," she stated.

He smiled at her. "Definitely not." His voice was soft and gentle.

"Who are you then?"

"My name is Ronin and I'm travelling alone, like you." The fire spat and the pot boiled up. "Come: you look hungry and I have a rabbit," he said as he crouched down on his haunches to stir the small black pot. Rhiannon didn't move, but watched him warily. There was no weapon anywhere to be seen. "You're quite safe," he said without looking up.

Rhiannon limped to a small rock, near enough to smell the food cooking, but not near enough to be reached. She stood there, unsure, with her hand resting on the hilt of her knife.

He glanced round at her. "You've hurt your foot?"

"Blisters."

Ronin nodded. "Painful." He filled a wooden bowl with stew; then carefully he put the spoon in it and placed it on the ground between them with a large hunk of bread. Then he stood a safe distance from her.

She collected the bowl then returned to the rock to eat. The heady smell of food overcame her fear and she ate it greedily, swallowing it down in great lumps. The delicacy of the flavour surprised her. They often ate rabbit at home, but this was different; full of roots and leaves with interesting flavours.

He watched her eat. When she had finished, he collected the bowl and filled it for himself. He shrugged. "I don't have visitors often," he explained. "I've just the one bowl."

They both smiled. Ronin closed his eyes and murmured something that sounded like the Latin her father sometimes tried to teach her. Then he ate. Rhiannon sat on the stone, watching him warily. She wondered what she must look like. Her hair was all snagged and pulled out into wild wisps from her plaits. Her cloak was ripped and her shoes were caked in mud. She must look like a beast, lost and broken.

Ronin stopped eating; his spoon held midway to his mouth. "Were you part of the boar hunt?" he asked. She nodded. "You've been separated from the others and are lost?" She nodded again. "By the time you get home, the settlement gates will be closed."

"How do you know all this?" Rhiannon asked, staring fiercely into his eyes.

He finished his stew, closed his eyes and mumbled to himself again. "I've been watching you all; keeping out of your way." Then he carried his bowl to the river and washed it out.

Rhiannon watched him walk away. He carries no weapon yet is unafraid to turn his back on me, she thought, nor has he asked for my knife.

After washing the bowl, Ronin washed his hands and face. He walked up the shingle towards Rhiannon. "You need to wash, too," he said.

Rhiannon swallowed hard and stared at the river. Her heart seemed to have stopped beating. It was true she was filthy, but the sun had now set, and Belisama would be waiting. She shuddered.

They both watched together as the moonlight rippled on the water. "You're worried Belisama will take you in the dark," he said. She nodded. "You've no silver nuts to placate her today, then?" Rhiannon stared at him, wide-eyed.

He brushed off a leaf from his brown cloak. "Well, if you fall in I'll have to pull you out again," he said, as he walked back towards a huge oak tree that stood on the edge of the wood.

Rhiannon followed him with her eyes, speechless. This must be the man who had pulled her out of the river.

TEN

A Shared Worry

There was a warm snugness to the root that served as a bed inside the hollow trunk of the old oak tree. It was worn smooth with use, and the sheep's wool blanket made it soft. Rhiannon sat on this earthy bed and combed out her matted hair with her fingers as best she could. She had washed her face in the river and rubbed her dirty boots clean. She felt better, but the knife in its sheath at her side still comforted her. Ronin sat outside the door, wrapped in a deer skin.

So he's not Brigantes, she thought to herself, *and he doesn't wear a torc.* She could just see the outline of his shoulder through the opening. "What tribe do you belong to?" she plucked up the courage to ask.

"Me?" Ronin queried as if there were someone else to answer. He stared up at the stars for a while, as if thinking. "I follow the way of Christ. So I am called a Christian. It's a sort of tribe."

"What's it like?"

"Well, we follow the teaching of our Father God and his Son, Jesus, the Christ. We believe that it is through Jesus that we know God, who teaches us how to live."

"Oh," Rhiannon said, feeling none the wiser.

A barn owl hooted as it flew silently between the trees. The sound filled Rhiannon with longings for home and the safety of the longhouse. She thought about her family worrying about her being out again at night and her eyes filled with tears. Her heart longed for Wolf with his reassuring soft fur. "I've never heard of your tribe," she said.

"No, I don't suppose you have. It's a pleasant one, though, of people who try to care for each other."

Rhiannon thought about this for a moment. "So why are you alone?" she asked.

"Some of my tribe were killed by the Saxons. I'm travelling to find another group of Christians in the east. I've been following the river. I'm staying here for the winter, until the weather is better and I can move on." He paused. "Or until my Father God moves me on again."

Rhiannon could just make out his head nodding in the moonlight. "Oh," she said again. She thought about the Saxons and her father's dread of them.

"May I ask you a question?" Ronin asked. "Why do you trust the silver nuts to protect you?"

Rhiannon shivered. "Well, Belisama lives in the river and she protects us as we hunt during the day. But at night it's different; then she wants souls to feed her and she takes those who wander."

Ronin nodded. "But why the silver nuts?"

Rhiannon snorted, indignantly. "All Brigantes know that Belisama will take the nuts instead."

"But do you trust her?"

Rhiannon thought for a moment. "I don't know; gods are hard to understand. My father does." The candle guttered, making the shadows dance like phantoms on the trunk walls. Rhiannon shivered. "The nuts aren't actually silver; they're polished iron. My brother makes them for his hunting trips and I sometimes take them with me."

"But not today?"

"No, I was supposed to stay with the group." For a moment, Rhiannon's thoughts turned back to the hunt. She couldn't remember when she'd last seen Wolf. What had her father meant about Pilot following Doran? Doran had been so worried about the hunt. She hoped he was back safely, now. Her father must have assumed she'd found the others and returned with them, too, or he would have been out looking for her.

Ronin interrupted her thoughts. "What if I told you Belisama doesn't exist?"

"That's silly; every Brigantes knows about Belisama. She stayed to help us when the Romans left. I hope she's going to help me." Rhiannon sighed. "She hasn't done yet, though."

She could hear Ronin chuckling. "Well, people in my tribe trust Father God. He is the only God there is. So, what do you want help with?" he asked.

"Well, it's not me really – it's Doran. I made a prayer on a lead sheet for him and threw it into the river, asking Belisama to help him. I think she doesn't help the poor. Perhaps she only helps those who can manage well for themselves."

Ronin nodded. "Like you and your family?"

"Yes," she said.

The wind moaned across the opening. Rhiannon could see Ronin pulling his deer skin up around his neck and over his head and then settle further into the crease in the trunk. "Why does Doran need prayer?" he asked.

"It's Torsa," she huffed. "You see, Doran's family are poor and his mother died. His father is cruel and Doran has to do everything or they'll starve. He does all the planting and hunting and looks after his little brother, Nico. He has no dog to help him because he can't get enough to feed one. If we try to help, Doran's father gets cross, and then Nico gets hurt. Now Torsa has started."

"What do you mean, Torsa has started? Started what?"

"Well, Torsa has been stealing Doran's rabbits. If we're doing training Torsa will go out of his way to hurt Doran, or make him look small. I caught him beating Doran behind one of the longhouses because he'd stood up to Torsa for once."

"He doesn't sound very kind, this Torsa."

"He's a bully!" Rhiannon blurted out. "Torsa has always been a bully. He thinks he's going to be a great warrior like his father. He despises Doran and his family because they once let the settlement down. There was some kind of fight, and people got hurt." Rhiannon closed her eyes, holding in the dreadful fear she felt. "That's why I asked Belisama to help us, but she didn't. In fact, it's only got worse. Yesterday my father said he thought he saw Pilot tracking Doran. Pilot is Torsa's dog. He's a great brute that could kill you. And Doran doesn't have a knife like I do." Rhiannon's hand instinctively checked for the knife on her belt. "Then when my father and I had cornered a great pig, I ended up being separated and now I'm lost." Despite herself she choked down a sob.

Ronin nodded. "I see. Well, I believe my God brought you here and he'll protect us both until morning. Then we shall take the coracle and row down to the settlement. Tonight, before I go to sleep, I'll ask Father God to help your friend."

"Don't you need lead sheet to put your prayers on?" she asked.

"No!" Ronin laughed. "I just talk. Now it's time for sleep."

He blew out the candle, and Rhiannon settled down into her bed of wool. Once in the dark, she noticed a red glow at the far side of the hollow. In front of it was the same wooden cross that Ronin wore around his neck. For some strange reason the glow behind the cross comforted her. She lay listening to Ronin talking in Latin. *Was that how he prayed?* she wondered, but very quickly exhaustion dragged her into a deep sleep.

When she woke up early next morning, Ronin wasn't there. Rhiannon squeezed herself through the opening and into the grey light before dawn. Stretching up to her full height she yawned and stretched. Her heart felt lighter, as though all her troubles had somehow been swept up and tidied away. Ronin was down by the river looking for something in the semi-dark. She limped down to join him.

"Did you sleep well?" he asked, smiling. She nodded. "Good, I'm looking for something I saw yesterday that you can take back with you."

She followed his gaze. "What are you looking for?"

"A stone." Ronin continued to search. "Yes, a dove stone! The dove is a symbol of peace. Ah, here it is!" He fished in the water, then held up the stone. It was mottled cream and white.

"It does look just like a dove!" Rhiannon exclaimed.

Ronin smiled and nodded. He placed it on her hand, and smiled again. They walked back slowly towards the tree. Rhiannon was still limping badly. "I'd better strap up that heel for you, so you can walk in your boots again."

Rhiannon flopped down onto the grass, leaning against the great oak, whilst Ronin mixed a balm for her foot. As she watched him, she thought how surprising it was that she trusted him so much, even though she didn't know him at all.

"It might sting a little," he said, as he rubbed the balm into the blister. "Feeling better?"

Rhiannon nodded. "Thank you."

Ronin placed sheep's wool over her heel and strapped it with a cloth. "Now you can put your boots back on." He looked up at the sky. "The sun's getting higher; we'd better get you back."

It wasn't long before they were both squashed into the coracle. Ronin had his face towards the rising sun. He only needed to use the oars occasionally to correct their drift, as the river took them along with the flow. Rhiannon sat opposite him, holding the dove stone on the flat of her palm. It felt cold against her skin. She ran her finger over its smooth surface, from the beak against her thumb across the raised wings covering her fingers.

She frowned as she looked back to the water. There was a pit of dread in her stomach as she thought of her parents worrying about her again. She looked up at Ronin, her face furrowed with a frown. He smiled, reassuringly. "I want you to take the dove stone with you, to remind you of Father God. Hold the stone and talk to him."

"So, do you do that?" Rhiannon looked unsure. "I don't remember you having a stone when you prayed."

Ronin smiled and fingered the cross around his neck. "No, but I do wear this cross to remind me." Then he looked up towards the sky and sighed while he thought. "God created each one of us and knows all about us. So he hears us if we pray. We don't need anything really. But I thought the stone would be something to remind you that he knows and hears, and he cares for you."

Rhiannon looked in puzzlement at the stone. "Why does your God care about me?"

"Father God cares about everything he's made. He loves us. I will pray for you and Doran and Torsa. For peace."

"Oh I see," said Rhiannon. But her brow was furrowed and her nose crumpled as she didn't really see at all. She turned the stone over in her hands, and as she turned it, she turned the new ideas about Father God over in her mind. Surely her father couldn't be wrong? Did Belisama really not exist? They travelled a little further in silence, listening to the splash of water against the side of the boat. Then they bumped against the bank.

"Are we home already?" Rhiannon blurted out and rewarded Ronin with a smile.

ELEVEN

Returning Home

"Easy, Wolf," Miriam said. She knelt by Wolf's side as he lay barely conscious on the dirt floor just inside the half-open gates.

Doran crouched next to them in the early morning light. The pain from his wounds almost overwhelmed him, and his damaged arm hung limply by his side. His face was grimy with blood and dirt and he was so, so tired.

He looked up with eyes that were painfully lost, as Silfor ran towards them. "I found Wolf," was all Doran said.

"Where?" Silfor asked quickly, bending down, as Miriam continued to stroke Wolf's matted fur. "Was Rhiannon with him?"

"No, he was alone. I found him in the woods as I was on my way back. He was in the bracken, half hidden. It was lucky I saw him in the dark."

Miriam looked up, tears in her eyes. "It's amazing how he got Wolf back. He's carried the dog home over his good shoulder; the other one's badly hurt. I came as soon as the gatekeeper called when he saw Doran struggling up the path."

As they spoke, villagers began gathering in a circle around Doran and Wolf. The men had their pikes with them. Nobody spoke.

"Doran!" a small voice called. "DORAN! DORAN!" With each repetition it was getting closer. Suddenly Nico forced his way through the growing the crowd until he reached his brother and then he clung to him, desperately. "Where were you all night?" Nico asked, gulping in great breaths of air. His small face was red and puffy from crying. "Where were you?" he repeated, wiping his dripping nose against his brother's trousers as he pushed his face hard against Doran's leg.

Doran gently rested his hand on Nico's hair and sighed deeply. "It's all right; I'm here now," he said wearily.

Leon pushed through the crowd and bent down next to his father when he saw Wolf. Gingerly he touched Wolf's flank. "What happened?" he demanded.

"He was trampled by the boar, I think," Doran replied, wincing in pain as he stood up.

Leon stroked the fur down Wolf's neck then felt him all over, listening carefully to the sharp intakes of breath and whimpers. "I don't think anything is broken. I think he's just badly bruised. So where's Rhiannon?"

Doran stroked Nico's head, perplexed. "Isn't she here?"

"No, and this is the second time Wolf's been badly hurt," Leon grumbled, his face creased by a deep frown. "This poor dog keeps giving himself up to protect her. He'll be lucky if he lives. Wasn't she with him?"

Doran shook his head. "No," he said.

Silfor placed his hand on Leon's shoulder, silencing his son's anger. "Take Wolf home to your mother." He turned to Doran. "We are about to make a search for Rhiannon."

Leon swept Wolf into his muscular arms, holding him gently like a child, and stood up. His face looked like thunder. Without a backward glance he walked away towards the longhouse, leaving Miriam on the ground alone. Doran pushed Nico away, wearily. "Go with him," he said. Nico let go of Doran's leg and ran after Leon and the dog.

Silfor helped Miriam up, then turned back to Doran. "Rhiannon didn't come home last night. I hoped you'd both found each other. We were just getting a search party together."

Doran looked round at the gathering villagers. "She wasn't with me. I thought she was hunting with you. I haven't seen her since we set off for the hunt."

Silfor grimaced. "We got separated. When I got back, Torsa said she was helping the women with the pigs, but I didn't check. This morning, when Maelbrigte joined them, she wasn't there."

"Torsa's a liar!" Doran spat out, unable to contain his anger any longer. "And he did this!" He pulled back his jerkin to reveal a jagged stripe across his shoulder where the arrow had scored him.

Governor Erdig stepped forward to take a closer look as Miriam gasped. "That needs to be cleaned," she said abruptly. "You'd better come home with me."

Silfor nodded and the men started talking all at once. Slowly, they made their way towards the gates, muttering grimly as they went. With a jolt Doran suddenly understood why the men were there. The men had their pikes ready to search the undergrowth. "I'll come with you," he called out.

Silfor turned to look at him. "No, get that shoulder sorted. Leave this to us," he said kindly.

Still, Doran hesitated; he looked round, unsure of what to do. His shoulder was aching terribly. Miriam pulled him gently but his feet were stuck. The men looked grim, preparing themselves for what they might find.

Suddenly, there was the faint sound of a girl's voice. A hush fell as they all strained to hear. Then it came again.

"Rhiannon!" Silfor shouted. Doran stepped forward, his heart pounding, his feet free at last. Silfor pushed his way through the men as he saw his daughter running up the path towards the gates. "Where have you been?" he demanded, as Rhiannon flung herself into his arms. "Praise be! Belisama has brought you home safely."

Doran ran his good hand through his dirty hair and breathed a sigh of relief. Rhiannon beamed at him over her father's shoulder. "I've been fine, Father," she said. "I've been safe and dry because I've had help."

Silfor hugged his daughter as they walk up the slope, almost squashing out her words.

"Who helped you?" Miriam asked, looking down the slope beyond the gates. Doran looked down towards the allotments and beyond. An early mist clung to the trees above the wood, but otherwise the morning was bright and clear. Pheasants scratched the earth by the path as usual, and the gorse waved lopsidedly in the wind, but there was no one to be seen. "Who helped you?" Miriam asked again. Doran looked at Rhiannon, wondering what she had meant, too.

Rhiannon hesitated, unsure how to explain. "I slept in a hollow oak tree."

"May Belisama be praised!" Silfor declared, hugging Doran as well as his daughter. "You are both home safe because she has protected you."

Doran winced with the pain from his shoulder. Miriam frowned. "We should be getting that shoulder seen to," she said.

"Why, what's happened to you?" Rhiannon asked.

Doran looked sadly at his friend. "Wolf's been badly hurt," was all he said.

Rhiannon blinked at him, speechless for a moment. "Wolf's hurt?" she asked. "Where is he?"

"Leon has taken him home," Silfor said. "It looks like he's been trampled on and bitten by the pigs. He's in a sorry way."

Rhiannon didn't wait to hear any more, but fled towards home. Doran stood watching her go until Miriam took hold of his hand to lead him away.

Behind him he heard Governor Erdig say to Silfor, "That girl has been fortunate again this time. We should look into

72

this trouble with Torsa, but I don't see how it can be true. Surely Doran is mistaken? Torsa wouldn't deliberately shoot him; he must have mistaken him for a boar."

Doran felt the old weight of despair settle on him again as he wearily walked away with Miriam. Why wouldn't anyone believe him?

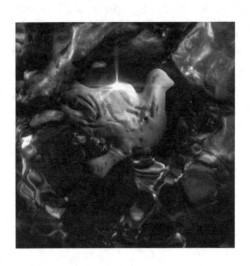

TWELVE

Answered Prayer

Rhiannon spent most of the day curled up beside the fire with Wolf, on a soft sheepskin Maelbrigte had brought for her, listening to Wolf's laboured breathing with a heavy heart.

She rubbed Wolf's soft fur between her fingers while she thought about what Leon had said earlier: "You don't deserve a noble dog like this; you are careless and thoughtless." His face had been taut with anger, unable to look at her. "You're headstrong and silly with no thought to the danger you're in. And no thought for our own parents' feelings, either," he'd ranted on.

Those words ran round and round in her head, chafing her. Wolf was hurt and she should have been there for him.

74

"I'm so sorry," she whispered to Wolf, rubbing her face in his flank, but he didn't even open his eyes. Rhiannon let her hand slide along Wolf's back. His fur looked clean and fresh but she knew underneath the skin was bruised and cut. "What happened to you?" she wondered, her eyes red and sore from crying.

Carefully, she looked at Wolf's neck and found the stitches Leon had made there. "Who made these cuts?" she wondered aloud. "Leon says they're too deep for pig bites." Gently she stroked him again and tears slid down her cheek. "I wish you could tell me."

Rhiannon picked up the balm that Leon had left and rubbed it into the skin around the stitches. Wolf whimpered and tried to pull away. Then she wrapped her arms round Wolf's neck and sobbed all over again. "Please forgive me for letting this happen to you."

As the day settled into evening, the owl on their roof hooted gently. Maelbrigte came to close the shutters of the open window. She smiled lovingly at her daughter before leaving her alone again. Rhiannon could see the red streak of the sunset through the gaps in the shutters. She thought again of the comforting glow of the light in Ronin's tree house the evening before, and pulled out the dove stone from the pocket on her belt. "Are you there, Father God?" she whispered. "Are you listening? Will you help?"

She turned the dove stone round in her hand as she thought about all that Ronin had said: that Belisama didn't exist and that his God heard her and cared for her. "Belisama hasn't made anything better. Will you help us?"

Clutching the dove stone tightly in her hand, she made

75

up her mind. "Father God, the God of Ronin, I have failed Wolf. He lies here hurt and dying because of my carelessness. I beg that you will heal him for his bravery."

After she had prayed, Wolf's eyes opened and his breathing slowly eased into a peaceful rhythm. He blinked slowly. Rhiannon stroked his head gently and Wolf licked at her fingers when they passed. Rhiannon started crying again, but this time with relief. "Thank you, thank you, Father God, God of Ronin," she whispered.

By morning Wolf was licking up small amounts of milk and wagging his tail. Leon came to check on Wolf before he went out to the forge. "I don't believe it!" he said to the dog in surprise. "I thought you would never recover! It's a miracle. We must praise the gods."

Rhiannon smiled and put her hand gratefully on the dove stone in her pocket. She knelt down by her brother. "Thank you for helping Wolf," she said, as he stroked the dog. Leon smiled at her. *Shall I tell him about Ronin and the stone?* Rhiannon wondered to herself, but the words dried up in her mouth. *He won't understand. Then they'll all just get angry about it and they might go and hurt Ronin.*

Maelbrigte smiled at Leon as she joined them. She knelt down, wrapping her arms around her daughter's shoulders. "Leave Wolf to rest now, he needs to sleep." As Leon went out to the forge, Maelbrigte pulled her daughter towards her, holding her tight. "Rhiannon, I know it wasn't your fault that you got separated," she said gently. "Your father blames himself. And Leon is just angry because he loves you and cares about your dog."

Rhiannon nodded, then with her head against her mother's shoulder, she sobbed again. The tears were for herself and Wolf; for the worry she had caused those she loved and the relief she felt to be home safe and sound.

While Wolf was sleeping, Rhiannon decided to take the dove stone to Doran. It had helped Wolf so it might just help him. As she walked down between the longhouses in the morning light, she thought about how wild Doran had looked at the gate. In her worry about Wolf she'd forgotten all about him. *I wonder what happened to Doran?* she thought. *He looked like he'd been beaten up. I wonder if he'd been hurt by the pigs like Wolf? Or by Torsa...*

As she reached the courtyard, she saw Miriam coming back from the allotments. "You look busy," Rhiannon called.

"I've been weeding," Miriam smiled. "I've done some sorting on Doran's patch, too. He'll not be doing heavy work for a while."

"What happened to him?"

Miriam moved a little closer. "Haven't you heard?" She took a deep breath. "Well, Doran said that when he broke cover into the field Torsa was standing with his longbow. He took aim and fired."

Rhiannon stared at her. "Torsa fired at Doran? Are you sure? Deliberately?"

Miriam nodded. "Doran says he did. He says Torsa saw him and then took aim." Rhiannon shook her head in horror, and Miriam looked all round before whispering, "Governor Erdig thought Torsa had been spooked into thinking Doran was a boar and had fired before he'd realised – but Doran is clear that Torsa had known it was him. The council are going to meet to discuss it."

"Weren't any of the other archers there?"

Miriam lowered her voice even further. "It seems not. Doran told me he just had time to drop to the ground, but the arrow still caught his shoulder. He pretended to be dead because he was terrified Torsa would come over and kill him."

Rhiannon shook her head again. "I know Torsa is mean, but surely even he wouldn't go that far?"

"Then the pigs arrived," Miriam continued. "Doran said he tried to get up but they trampled all over him. He was in a real mess."

Rhiannon's lip trembled a little as she asked. "Is that when Wolf saved him?"

"I don't think so," Miriam said, looking perplexed. "I don't remember him saying anything about Wolf saving him. How is Wolf?"

Rhiannon sighed. "We think he's going to be all right. But I don't think he'll ever be as strong as he once was."

Miriam nodded. The two girls stood silently for a moment, then Miriam squeezed her hand. "He's a brave warrior, that dog of yours."

"I know. I don't deserve him."

Rhiannon didn't really like going to Doran's hut, in case Jago was there, so she was relieved when Miriam told her that Doran and Nico were staying in Governor Erdig's longhouse until Doran had regained his strength. As she made her way there, she hardly noticed the chickens scratching about around her on the path. *If I give Doran the stone in the longhouse, I'll have to explain to Governor Erdig about Ronin*, she thought. *No one has asked me to explain about how I survived that night. What if Governor Erdig doesn't understand and sends out men to find Ronin?*

She still hadn't made up her mind about what she'd say when she reached the longhouse, so she sat on the porch, swinging her legs and thinking. Governor Erdig's dog, Juniper, flopped his massive body down at her feet, like a cushion for a king. He smelt strongly now of old dog, but she bent down to ruffle his torn ear. Nico wasn't far behind him – he came and sat down next to her with a smile.

"How's Doran?" she asked, as he placed his feet on Juniper's brown back.

"He's getting better. He's asleep now. Is Wolf getting better?" Nico asked.

Rhiannon nodded. "Yes."

"Has it made you sad? You look sad."

"Do I?" Rhiannon forced a weary smile and hugged Nico. "He must have been looking for me," she explained, "so that makes me feel sad. I don't know what I'd do without Wolf."

Nico nodded. "Sometimes I feel sad, too."

Rhiannon made up her mind. "I've got a stone," she said. "It looks like a dove." She pulled the stone out of her pocket and showed it to Nico. Nico gasped and took it between his fingers.

"It does look like a dove. I've never seen a stone that looks like a bird before; it even has a beak!" he said.

The pair stared at the stone for a moment. "I think it helped Wolf get better when I prayed with it," Rhiannon said.

Nico frowned. "Why would Belisama listen to your stone? I've never used a stone. Does it work like the silver nuts?"

"I didn't pray to Belisama – or to the stone," Rhiannon replied. She looked up at the soft clouds floating over the blue sky, as she sorted her thoughts. "I met someone in the wood. His name is Ronin. He's part of a different tribe called Christians and he's trying to find more of his people. He told me about his Father God and he gave me this stone. Ronin says that his God loves us and cares about us. He helps us if we pray. He gave me the stone to remind me."

Nico looked at her, wide-eyed. "You talked to the man in the woods?"

Rhiannon nodded. "Yes, I did."

"Weren't you scared?"

"No. Well a bit, at first. He was kind and I felt I could trust him. He was the one who pulled me out of the river, that other time."

Nico weighed the stone in his hand. "And he says this bird stone will help us?"

"Well, not exactly. He says that we just have to hold the stone and ask his Father God for help," she said. "The dove stone just reminds us. It's the God who gives the help."

Nico looked closely at the stone. "Do you think it would help Doran to get better?" he asked. "He's very angry and tired."

Rhiannon smiled at him. "I think it's worth a try." She took hold of Nico's hand so that the stone was caught between their palms. "Father God, God of Ronin, please will you make Doran well?"

"And stop Torsa hurting him," Nico added. Rhiannon nodded in agreement. They sat together, quietly, for a moment.

Rhiannon looked hard at Nico. "Do you think you could give Doran the stone and tell him how to use it? But you mustn't show it to anyone else. They won't understand." She looked pointedly towards the longhouse. Nico nodded. "You won't forget, will you?"

Nico put the stone in his pocket, hugged Rhiannon and skipped back into the longhouse. Juniper stood up and followed him. "Well, I hope it works," Rhiannon whispered to herself.

THIRTEEN

Run For Your Life

Two days later Doran returned home. He had told Governor Erdig that he was strong enough. "If I'm not there, things get on top of me," he said. "I need to be getting on again."

Governor Erdig had agreed and his wife had packed some food for the boys to live on for the first few days. "Just until you get yourselves sorted," she'd said with a smile. "You can always come back if you need more."

"I've told Torsa we're watching him, so you should have no more trouble," Governor Erdig added. "It's time to move on and put this unpleasantness behind us."

Doran said nothing, but he didn't believe Torsa would leave him alone.

For all the warmth and safety of Governor Erdig's longhouse, Doran was glad to get home. It wasn't until he was making up the fire that Nico remembered the dove stone and took it out of his pocket. "What have you got there?" Doran asked.

"Nothin'."

Doran held out his hand. "Give it here."

"It's a stone, that's all," Nico said sulkily, placing the stone into Doran's palm.

Doran looked closely at it. "It looks like a dove; I wonder where it's from?"

Nico shrugged. "Rhiannon gave it to me."

Doran turned the stone over. "Why did she give it to you?"

"It's to pray with," Nico said simply.

Doran placed the stone into the pocket on his belt and smiled at Nico for the first time since the hunt. Nico smiled back and felt a little flutter of happiness. Perhaps everything would go right now.

Later that evening, Doran sat by the fire with the stone in his hand. It felt smooth and warm as he ran his finger along the grooves in its shape. He didn't understand why the stone comforted him, but it did. His shoulder was beginning to ease and he rolled it back stiffly. *Belisama must have sent this stone*, he thought. *In the morning I'll dip it into the water when I go to the allotment, to thank her.*

Next morning, Doran was out early on the allotment. It had taken him a while to rouse Nico, who was still yawning, even as they worked. "Put your back into it," Doran scolded, but Nico always daydreamed more than he worked. He

83

pushed the hoe at the soil, but more often than not it just skittered across the surface.

"Morning," Miriam called as she reached her strip, near theirs. "I didn't expect to see you so soon."

Doran smiled, but said nothing. Nico took the opportunity to stop work. "He's not well enough, really. He ought to be resting, so I said I'd come and help."

Miriam smiled. "You don't look like you're helping much."

"I'm going to hoe this side while Doran gets those seedlings weeded and spaced out. He thinks someone's been doing some work here already."

Miriam looked over towards Doran. "That was me," she said.

Doran smiled at her and nodded his thanks.

"What was it like living with Governor Erdig?" Miriam asked. Then Nico was off, talking fast about the comforts of living in Governor Erdig's longhouse. He'd been amazed at the wonderful things he'd been given to eat, but moaned about having to sit up at the table to eat them. Nico rested on his hoe as he chatted while Miriam worked in front of him and Doran worked behind.

Very soon it became clear that what had impressed Nico the most was Governor Erdig's dog, Juniper. "He's just so old," Nico explained. "He spends his days sleeping. I don't believe all those stories about how he's taken down boars on his own. He's far too fat; and he snores. I'm sure he couldn't have been such a famous warrior."

Miriam grinned at Doran over the top of Nico's head.

Nico sighed. "I think he only woke up when he had to find me. Then he'd drag me out for a wash or something nasty like that. I was always having to wash! I don't know how he always knew where I was. If I didn't move quickly enough, he'd start growling and showing his teeth." Despite the complaints Nico smiled, wistfully. "I wouldn't mind," he concluded, "but he kept nipping my bottom. My breeches are worn thin with it. You'd think he'd have better manners."

"And here's me thinking that it's all that squirming about you do," Miriam said, smiling broadly. Doran smiled at Nico's tale, but it didn't fill the emptiness he still felt inside.

They all worked hard for a while. Some time later, when Doran looked up, Miriam was ready to go and she waved as she set off back to the settlement.

"We'd better go, too," Doran said, a few minutes later, as the last seedling went in. "The fish traps by the river need emptying. I'll be quicker on my own; you go back with Miriam. Hurry and you'll catch her up."

Nico nodded and set off at a run.

The traps were empty. Doran sighed in disappointment. But there was something else he wanted to do while he was alone by the river. He took the dove stone from his pocket. "Hail, mighty Belisama," he whispered. "Thank you for the stone. Please help me with Torsa." The cold water streamed past his feet and a sudden gust of wind made him shudder.

As he turned to go, his stomach lurched. Pilot was standing in the middle of the grassy path, blocking his way. Torsa stood close behind him and in his right hand he held Nico by his jerkin.

Doran's legs felt like jelly and his hoe fell to the floor with a rattle. He stood there, watching Nico's thin legs swinging in the air.

"I believe this is yours. He stinks of rat," he heard Torsa hiss, before spitting into Nico's face. Torsa looked into Doran's eyes and Pilot growled. "I want you to know this," continued Torsa. "My arrow won't miss next time. I'll finish what I started." Torsa poked a long, menacing finger into Nico's shoulder to make sure they both understood. "Perhaps I'll let the dog have this one," he said as he threw Nico face down on the ground. Doran couldn't move; fear paralysed him. "Pathetic creatures," Torsa spat. "Come, dog. We'll leave the dung where it belongs."

With that, Torsa turned and walked back towards the settlement, with Pilot following him. The tightness round Doran's chest almost crushed him. Nico lay sobbing at his feet. Doran knelt down next to his little brother and placed his hand gently onto his back. "It's all right. They've gone now."

Nico scrambled into a ball by his knees and sucked his thumb. "They hate us," he said, around it. "They're going to kill us."

Doran stroked Nico's hair. His eyes were grave as he looked towards the gates, his heart black with despair. After a while, Nico stopped crying and he sat up. Doran's face was set. "We must leave," was all he said.

Panic furrowed Nico's face. "But where will we go?"

Doran didn't explain. He offered no smile, no shrug, no hopeful gesture. "I'll need my pike," he said. "And we'll need our cloaks if we're going to travel."

Doran took Nico by the hand and the pair walked back up the path towards the settlement, forgetting all about the hoe. But as they neared the gate they saw Pilot, resting against the far gate post with his head upon his paw. For all the world he looked like he was sleeping peacefully. His eyes were closed and his breath was slow. It was only the alertness of his ears that warned that he was waiting for them.

"We'll not get past," Doran whispered in panic. "He won't let us in."

At that, Doran turned and fled, dragging Nico behind him. The two boys raced down the rise, past the allotments and on toward the woodland and the river. "Where will we sleep?" Nico wanted to know, his small hand trembling in Doran's larger one.

"We'll find somewhere," was Doran's gruff reply.

"Will we have anything to eat?" Nico panted.

"No."

"Will we be off the ground?"

"Probably not."

"Will a boar find us?"

"No."

"Will anyone come and help us?"

"Just be quiet," Doran snapped.

By the time they reached the river the sun was going down behind them. Ahead of them the water sparkled in the last rays of the day. From the settlement came a long low howl like the sound of a great bear. "That's Juniper," Nico said.

Doran ground his teeth. "What would you know?"

They followed the bank of the river. Doran had no plan; no idea of what they could do or where they could go. But he was absolutely sure that they couldn't return. His thoughts about Torsa chased round and round in his mind, filling him with dread.

Nico stumbled along beside him. "Are you going to dip the stone?"

Doran shivered. "No. Belisama doesn't listen to the likes of us."

It wasn't long before Doran noticed a cradle of branches in an old tree. The hollow was full of leaves and moss and there was just enough room for one person to sleep within it. "Up you go," Doran said. As Nico climbed in, he added, "Now be quiet and no one will know you're there."

Doran sank down and sat at the base of the tree. He hugged his knees to himself. He had never felt so alone. He had no plan and no hope. Tears slid down his cheeks like helpless snowflakes destined to melt away.

FOURTEEN

Rhiannon to the Rescue

The ceiling of the longhouse slowly lightened as dawn arrived. Wolf lay awake on the end of Rhiannon's bed, waiting for the first signs of the new day. He heard Juniper's call and gently licked Rhiannon's fingers and snuffled her neck as she lay sleeping on her bed. "It's too early," she complained. "Go back to sleep."

Wolf licked her fingers again, giving the little one a nip. Rhiannon sat up, rubbing her eyes with the heel of her hand. "What's the matter?"

Wolf was off. He trotted to the head of the stairs then paused and looked back at her. Rhiannon got out of bed and walked towards him. Wolf immediately clattered down the stairs and stood facing the door with his head lowered, his hind quarters quivering anxiously. Bewildered, Rhiannon looked at him as the first rays of the sun stretched across the room. Suddenly she made up her mind. "OK, I'll get dressed." Wolf's tail wagged hard.

A few minutes later she was fully dressed and wrapped in her cloak. She tip-toed down the stairs, checking that her knife was secure on her belt. Her dark hair was braided neatly down her back ready for action, and her pale face was thoughtful and drawn with the uncertainty. She patted Wolf. "I wish you could tell me what's wrong." She stroked his head and he leaned gently against her.

Better take some food, she thought, suddenly. Rhiannon collected a drinking flask of water from the kitchen. She placed a large hunk of bread and some cheese in her pocket and fastened it on her belt. She stood for a moment, checking she had all she needed, then whirled round and returned to Wolf, collecting her pike from by the door as she left.

Minutes later the pair were striding down the lane. She could hear Leon and her dad in the forge, but she didn't stop to tell them where she was going. She didn't really know herself.

She followed Wolf through the settlement until they reached Doran's hut. Peering warily in, Rhiannon could see that it was empty. *Nothing but rats*, she thought as she peered through the doorway. *Where are Doran and Nico?* she wondered with a start, looking at Wolf. The dog barked and turned full circle.

The long horn sounded sharp and clear to announce the gates would be opening. It was followed by a long low howl from Juniper. Wolf threw back his head and howled in response. Rhiannon looked anxiously at her dog – he'd never behaved like this before. Then it hit her with a thump: Doran and Nico were outside, and they were in danger.

As the long horn announced the dawn, Doran was hunched on a stone by the river. The water was oily and black as it swirled past his feet. In the half-light, the river sang soulfully of endless darkness. All he had to do was to allow himself to sink within her grasp and he would be free of the leaden blackness in his heart.

"Doran," the high-pitched voice trembled in fear. "DORAN!"

"I'm by the river."

Doran could hear Nico scrambling and sliding towards him. Soon the small quivering body was crouched against his side. "Doran? What are we going to do? Have you dipped the stone?"

Doran's whole body flooded with hopelessness. "I've already told you: Belisama won't help the likes of us. All she'll do is take our souls.

"But we must try," Nico pleaded. "Rhiannon said we should."

Doran reached into his pocket and pulled out the stone. He held it out in the palm of his hand. Reverently, Nico stroked the wings of the dove, his dirty face streaked with tears. "Please help us, dove," he whispered.

Rage filled Doran. "We might as well just throw it away. Nobody is going to help us now!"

Wolf galloped into the main yard and trotted over to the gate. Painfully, Juniper stood up from his place near the gatepost; he was getting too old to be out all night. The two dogs greeted each other, their noses touching.

"You're all up early," the gatekeeper said to Rhiannon in surprise as he fastened the gates.

Rhiannon pulled herself to her full height and stared at him. "I'm going out and I'm taking Wolf with me." She'd promised her mother she'd be careful – and now she was going out again. Should she go or should she stay safe? But Wolf was already searching for Nico's scent on the dry earth outside the gates. His ears were pricked forward and his tail in the air as he searched.

"What's he after?" the gatekeeper asked. Suddenly, there it was. Wolf gave a small sharp bark and was off on their trail. Rhiannon had no choice but to follow. "Does your mother know?" the gatekeeper called after them.

Rhiannon kept running, her pike in her hand. "Tell her I've gone fishing," she shouted.

They ran past the allotments until they could see the long grey snake of the river. They stopped by the river bank for a moment, panting, then ran on again. Rhiannon shielded her eyes from the glare of the morning sun and searched the land ahead. After a while she made out two small figures by the river. "There they are!"

Wolf ran on in front and Rhiannon picked up her pace, trying to keep up. Down the bank they hurried, skirting the edge of the wood. Wolf was soon at full gallop along the river bank, slithering to a stop when he got to Doran and Nico. The dog sniffed and snuffled around Nico, checking him over. "It's all right," Nico laughed, as he stroked Wolf in return.

Rhiannon's face was bright red and covered in sweat when she finally caught up. She bent over, resting her hands on her thighs as she dragged in great gulps of air. "That dog can certainly run," she gasped.

Once Rhiannon had got her breath back, they all settled on a fallen trunk to eat the food she'd brought. Nico grabbed at the bread, stuffing it into his mouth. "Doran's hungry, too," Rhiannon scolded, as she took some of it back.

Wolf walked slowly to the river for a drink and Nico followed him, playing with the pebbles at its edge. Doran sat hunched, unable to look at Rhiannon. After a while he asked, "Why have you come?"

Rhiannon touched his shoulder gently. "To take you back."

Doran's eyes filled with tears. "We can't go back. Torsa wants to kill us."

"You have to come back. You'll die out here, outside the settlement."

Doran turned his face away from her. "Better my chances with the boar than with Torsa."

Angrily, Rhiannon stood up. "What about Nico?" she demanded.

Doran looked her in the face. "You can take him back with you." Doran pulled out the stone and held it out to Rhiannon. "I've asked Belisama to help us but it's hopeless. I'm hopeless. I can't even feed us properly. Take Nico to Governor Erdig; they'll look after him. I'll make myself a place away from here. I'll be all right on my own."

Rhiannon began to cry. "You can't live alone, Doran. We can't let Torsa win. We just can't. You have to come back and we have to make it right."

Rhiannon took the stone from Doran's palm. She held it firmly in her fist and breathed in deeply. "Father God, God of Ronin, we need your help," she prayed aloud. "Please show us what to do."

Doran stared at her. "Who is Father God, and who is Ronin?"

Rhiannon glared at Nico, but he was too busy playing to notice. "Ronin saved me from Belisama when I got lost in the night. He pulled me out of the river when I thought she'd take my soul. Then he helped me when I got lost in the forest after the boar hunt. He doesn't believe in Belisama. He says there is only one God and he cares for us. He gave me the stone, to remind me to pray to him. I gave it to Nico to give to you . . ."

Suddenly, Nico was at her side. "Do you think your friend would help us?"

Rhiannon looked down at him and smiled. "Yes, I think he would. He lives further up the river. Well, I think it's further on." She peered along the river bank ahead of them.

Doran looked amazed. "Why would he help me? Do you trust him?"

"Yes, I do trust him. He saved my life, remember?"

FIFTEEN

The Big Decision

They decided to walk up the river, because although Rhiannon couldn't remember exactly where she had stayed that night, she was certain it couldn't be too far away. As they walked, she told Doran all about the night after the hunt, then added, "The trouble is, if Ronin doesn't want to be seen, I think he just hides." She kicked a pebble and it flew in a long arc, landing in the river with a loud plop.

"I wish Torsa was gone," Nico said. "He picked me up and said he'd let Pilot eat me."

"Well, that's just wicked!" Rhiannon exclaimed.

"I told you," said Doran. "We can't go back. He intends to finish us off."

A deep voice came from behind them. "Who is it you are afraid of?"

Rhiannon jumped and Nico grabbed Doran's leg for safety, but Wolf went and sat on his rump in front of the brown clad man. His tail wagged against the earth, making a smooth, flat semi-circle. He looked completely at ease.

"Hello, old friend," Ronin said. He leaned forward, stroking Wolf's head while he cupped the dog's chin in the palm of his other hand. "You're a true friend to these lost souls."

Rhiannon watched Wolf in bewilderment for a moment. "He's remembered you!" she cried. "When you saved me from the river you saved him, too!"

Ronin looked up and smiled. "I guess that's true."

"We've been looking for you," she said.

"I know," Ronin nodded, "I've been listening."

Then they were all talking at once. It wasn't long before Ronin knew all about Torsa and how his treatment of Doran made him feel helpless and alone; and how Nico was frightened of losing his brother.

"I think we need some food," Ronin said, hearing Nico's stomach rumbling. "I have some rabbits. Shall we cook them on sticks and think about what we can do?"

Rhiannon held Nico's hand as they walked back downstream to find Ronin's camp. They'd missed it completely as they'd stumbled along by the river. Soon the fire was glowing again and they all had meat on a stick to roast over the embers.

"I've been thinking about your troubles," Ronin said. "Facing something that frightens us so much that we run away is hard. You must feel that no one in the settlement will listen or can help. But I know a story that might encourage you."

"Does it have mystical creatures in?" Nico asked.

Ronin shook his head, chuckling. "No. Only people. There were once two great peoples: the tribe of Israel and the tribe of the Philistines. The Israelites belonged to God but the Philistines – well, they just loved fighting, and they wanted to take the land that belonged to the tribe of Israel. One day the Philistines arrived and their famous giant soldier, whose name was Goliath, offered a challenge. If an Israelite could defeat him in a duel, then the Philistines would spare them. If Goliath won, the Philistines would take their land. The Israelite soldiers were all terrified.

Now, in the hills was a shepherd boy called David. He heard about this towering Goliath but, unlike all the Israelite soldiers, he wasn't afraid. He believed that his Father God would help him defeat the Philistine. So he left his sheep, took some small round stones and went to face Goliath.

Everyone thought David was foolish, because he was just a boy. Goliath laughed when he saw David and he picked up his sword to slay him. But David put a stone in his sling, swirled it round and slung it. The stone struck Goliath in the centre of his forehead, and he fell.

The Israelites were thrilled. They chased the Philistines away and eventually that shepherd boy became their king."

When Ronin had finished his story, Nico asked, "So, should we throw stones at Torsa?"

"No, we don't need to hurt Torsa; that's not the point," Ronin said with a smile. "The important thing was that

David trusted God. That gave him the courage he needed to fight the giant, with the things he was good at using."

Rhiannon frowned and asked, "So Doran should fight Torsa?"

"What I'm thinking is, Torsa might back down if he sees that you're not afraid any more," Ronin said. "The important thing was that David trusted his Father God, who gave him courage to face the giant. That's what you need to think about."

"How do I know this Father God of yours will help me?" Doran asked, frowning. "He might be like Belisama. She promises help – but never does."

"I don't believe in Belisama," Ronin said.

Nico looked up in surprise and asked: "What about Gobannus? Torsa has him on his belt."

"Not Gobannus either," Ronin added.

Rhiannon gasped. Her father trusted Gobannus for his work; all metal workers did.

"There is only one God who made our world," Ronin continued. "He loves us and wants us to know him. He is the one who can help you. Has he helped you so far?"

"Well, he brought us to you when Rhiannon prayed," Nico acknowledged. He stared at Rhiannon, looking for reassurance and she smiled back at him.

"Hmm, maybe that's true," Doran said grudgingly. Nico snuggled closer to him. Rhiannon looked across at them, trying to decide whether to speak or not. The breeze fluttered and fretted at her cloak, pulling against the circular pin at her neck.

"When Wolf was dying, I prayed and Father God healed him," she said at last. "Even Leon thought it was a miracle. I've asked your God to keep Doran safe from harm, too."

Wolf gave a large sigh and they all looked at him as he lay curled up by Rhiannon's side.

"Well, Doran has been kept safe from harm so far. I've been asking my Father God to help Doran too," said Ronin. "And look: here we all are together."

"Why did you pray for me?" Doran asked in surprise.

"Well, we Christians believe in showing God's love. For me part of that means praying for people I meet and telling them all about how Father God can help them. I've been praying for you since Rhiannon told me about your struggles with Torsa."

Silence settled on them all, like leaves falling from the trees in autumn, as they turned over this idea in their minds. "My rabbit's burning," said Nico suddenly, breaking the silence and snatching at his stick and gobbling up his meat. The others ate their rabbit, thinking about what Ronin had said.

When they'd finished the delicious meat, Rhiannon watched Doran get up and walk across to the river. He looked so small and helpless by the vast expanse of water. She followed him and stood by his side. A tiny dipper hopped onto a flat rock in front of them. It bobbed up and down as if bowing. Doran smiled at her.

"We can do it together," Rhiannon said. "You don't have to be alone with this."

Doran shuffled about awkwardly, looking down at his feet. Silently, Wolf came and sat between them as they watched the river sparkling. "Do you believe this Father God of Ronin's can help us?"

She watched the droplets from the splashing water fall back into the river. "I think so."

Doran followed her gaze. "You can see a rainbow in them," he said, the tension dropping from his face.

"Let's go back together and face Torsa," Rhiannon said. Doran looked at her and nodded.

SIXTEEN

The Stand Off

"So the problem about going back is that Torsa's dog, Pilot, is guarding the gate?" Ronin asked.

"He was yesterday. We need to get past him if we want to talk to Governor Erdig," Doran answered.

"Well, what will give you the courage to deal with the dog?"

Doran sat in silence, fiddling with the straps of his shoe while he thought. He pushed his finger into another hole that had formed in the sole. "I'm not sure."

"What would you take with you if you went fishing?"

"That's easy," interrupted Nico. "He uses his pike." Then quick as a flash, the boy was on his feet sticking out his bottom and wriggling it, an imaginary pike in his hand. "He's as quick as a wink," he said, as he stabbed an imaginary fish.

Doran nodded. "Yes, the pike. I can use a pike."

"Well, that's what you take. Then you have something with you if Pilot is guarding the gate. Go to Governor Erdig first and get help to sort this out. But if you meet Torsa on your way, try to talk to him, to change his mind. Get others in the settlement to tell him also. Father God often uses other people to help us."

Despair washed over Doran again. "I haven't got my pike. Mine is still in the settlement because of Pilot."

"You could use mine," Rhiannon offered, holding her pike out towards Doran. He stood up and took it in his hand, weighing it. It was light and a bit short for him. He tossed it from hand to hand but it didn't feel right at all. Doran frowned.

"Would mine be better?" Ronin offered.

Doran wasn't at all sure but the look of trust on Rhiannon's face persuaded him, settling the panic that he felt. He looked hard at Ronin and realised that he trusted him, too. "Can I see it?" he asked.

He followed Ronin back up the beach towards the oak tree, leaving the others to wait by the fire.

The small opening in the trunk of the tree looked like a secret door. Just inside was a long heavy stick with a pointed end. While Ronin stooped to reach it Doran glimpsed inside. No stink of rat here. Although the floor was made of packed earth it was swept clean and covered in sweet smelling grass. A twisted root had been fashioned into a bed with a covering of soft sheepskin.

"A good safe home is a gift from God, so I keep it well," Ronin said, noticing Doran's look of approval.

Doran nodded. "If I get through this," he said, "things will be different."

Ronin handed Doran the pike. "It's sharp," he said, "but perhaps a little too long for you?"

Doran balanced the pike across the palm of his hand, testing its weight. "It's not too bad, just a little heavy away from its point."

Ronin nodded. "That's because I've trimmed it to the spike, keeping the weight to the other end. It makes it more useful if I need to defend myself."

Doran walked away, swinging the pike in great arcs and feeling how the weight changed with the movement. He noticed the balance of its length and the usefulness of the weight being more at one end.

Nico kicked at Rhiannon's foot, and she leaned up on one elbow in the sand, watching him.

"It is well balanced once you're used to it," Doran said. He came to a stop, his feet wide apart and his back straight, then he swung the pike up and over his shoulder ready to throw. With a deep grunt he launched it up the river bank in a monstrous arc until it landed with a sharp thud in the ground where it stood quivering. "It's good," Doran said. "More than good. It's better than mine."

Ronin smiled. "Just remember to return it. I will need it for fishing!"

The sun had reached its highest point in the sky as the little group prepared to return to the settlement. Rhiannon refilled her flask with fresh water for the journey back, while

Nico played hide and seek with Wolf round the trees. Ducks swam happily in and out of the water's edge, but when Wolf came snuffling along, they took to the air in a flurry of quacking and squawking. Madly flapping their wings, they trailed their webbed feet along the wet surface.

"See how they run!" Nico said, holding his sides with laughter.

Doran watched them and smiled sadly. *I have to go back,* he thought. *Nico needs me.*

"Hopefully Pilot won't be there," Ronin said, "then you can all go and talk to your Governor – explain what happened. Remember: use the pike to defend yourself only if you have to."

The friends nodded. Doran's hand searched for the dove stone to check it was still in his pocket. He needed to know that this God of Ronin's was still with them.

"Won't you come with us?" Doran asked. Nico stopped and looked at Ronin, too.

"I'll come to the edge of the wood," Ronin said. "This is your battle. I'll find myself a quiet spot and pray for you."

Doran nodded. He started to lead the way back along the river but his pace was too slow for Nico, who was soon skipping ahead with Wolf. Ronin lagged behind, his face deep in thought. Behind him Doran heard Rhiannon ask, "What are you thinking about?"

"I was thanking God," he said, "Thanking him for this chance to help you all. And I was asking him to give you courage."

It didn't seem to take long to get back to familiar territory. Soon they could see the allotments and the walls of the settlement standing proudly before them, like a dark hat on the head of the hill.

"Trust in God and take courage," Ronin said, at the edge of the woods. "Remember he goes with you. There is no other God but him."

Rhiannon nodded and Doran reached for the dove stone in his pocket as they listened to the prayer Ronin said quietly for their safety. *Please help us*, Doran thought anxiously. Then he realised it was more than a thought. It was a prayer.

As the group started up the rise, a flock of pheasants drifted off the allotments and gathered round them. Their round fat bodies looked full of confidence as they strutted along. Nico laughed, and Doran smiled, but when he looked up his stomach lurched as if a blow had crushed the air out of him. He stopped dead. Right ahead of them, in the middle of the gateway, stood Pilot.

"What shall we do?" Rhiannon breathed.

"We should go back down and think," Doran whispered, his legs trembling.

But then Nico caught a peahen with his foot. She squawked suddenly, madly flapping her wings as she tried to get off the ground. Then all the other pheasants took off in a great panic of noise and flapping.

Pilot ignored the birds and looked directly at Doran. He made a long low growl and moved a few steps forward. Without a sound Nico slipped his hand into Rhiannon's. Pilot snarled, showing his sharp white teeth. A slobber of drool dripped slowly from his jaw.

"Too late to run now," Doran whispered. He thought of the stone but couldn't move to touch it. Pilot lowered his head, ready to charge. Wolf paced forward, his feet four square. Then he threw back his head and howled. The whole world seemed to stop and into the silence one single splat of drool hit the ground from Pilot's jaw.

A faint answering howl drifted from inside the settlement. Pilot's ears twitched and he took a step forward.

Wolf matched him.

A second howl came from the settlement, nearer this time. Juniper was on his way. Wolf moved forward and bared his teeth. He let out a low, menacing growl. Pilot matched him. Then Juniper rounded the gate behind Pilot like a lone crusader, his scarred face set in determination and his ears flapping like torn flags knotted to a mast.

Pilot sprang into the air towards Doran like a bullet from a gun, but Wolf pounced at the same time and the two dogs slammed into each other in mid-air.

Pilot sunk his teeth into Wolf's neck. Holding him hard he threw Wolf to one side, his eyes still on Doran. Wolf swirled round as his feet brushed the ground, blood oozing from his wound. Juniper joined in, pouncing onto Pilot's back, unsteadying him but failing to knock him over. Then Wolf sprang at the soft flesh of Pilot's neck, pulling him to the ground.

Even on the ground Pilot kept Doran in his sights. Wolf kept his hold on Pilot's neck as his feet scrabbled at the packed earth. Then Juniper tore into Pilot's leg, leaving a gaping wound. Pilot tried to stand but failed; his leg was paralysed. Rhiannon and Nico clung together, staring at the fighting dogs in horror.

Then, walking calmly through the middle of the gates, came Torsa. He stood behind the fighting dogs. In his hand he held the training sword, and his eyes were locked on Doran.

SEVENTEEN

The Breach

Leon leaned against the door jamb of the forge with his arms folded across his chest. "Is Rhiannon back?"

"No," Silfor said. Silfor had his back to his son as he hammered the bright red bar that he'd just pulled from the charcoal.

"The gatekeeper said she left at first light with Wolf," Leon added. "He thought she was going fishing as she had her pike. And food in a pocket! I hope she hasn't gone to the other side of the river again."

Silfor stopped hammering and then turned the bar, looking at it carefully. "She promised me she wouldn't," he said, without looking up.

"You know what she's like, though."

Silfor turned to face his son. "Actually, she reminds me of you."

A deep frown furrowed Leon's face. "One day she might get really hurt."

Silfor turned and plunged the flattened iron bar into the charcoal. "Be useful and get those bellows going."

Leon bent over the wooden beam, cranking it down. Immediately, the charcoal brightened and gave out an intense heat. He sighed. "I just want her to be safe."

"She's strong and she's fearless. I'd rather have your sister by my side than many men in the settlement."

Leon smiled. "I know she's fast, but she's also reckless."

"She'll learn, like you did. If she's strong enough to forge her own knife she's strong enough to hunt her own meat."

Silfor put down his tools, took off one gauntlet and scooped up a mug of water. Then he poured it over his head to cool himself.

At that moment they caught the sound of a dog howling from the other side of the settlement.

Silfor frowned, turning his ear towards the gates. "What was that? It sounded like Wolf. I'd know that howl anywhere."

Then there was an answering howl. "That's Juniper! Why would Juniper be howling now?" Leon asked, looking down the track towards the main yard.

Silfor started to hang up his tools. "Something must be up." He wiped his hands on a rag, then together they ran towards the yard, their leather aprons flapping with each step.

As they came into the main yard they stopped. The square was eerie and quiet, with not a soul to be seen. A dried leaf spun across the floor, chased by the wind. "Where is everyone?" Leon asked.

"Where's the gatekeeper?" Silfor asked. "He should always be here." Another howl split the silence. "That was definitely Wolf – and it came from outside the gate."

Leon looked towards the gateway and started to run towards it. Silfor looked back up the way they had come. Running down the middle of the track was Maelbrigte. "Silfor, Leon!" she called as she ran.

"What's the matter?" Silfor asked.

Maelbrigte stood for a moment with her hands on her knees as she steadied her breathing. Her hands and forearms were stained the colour of mud from the tanning. "You must come," she said. "The tanning tank has split and the mixture is leaking. We've pushed the old gate panel against it and the men are trying to hold it."

"That won't last," Leon said, running back towards the forge.

"We'll need the long braces," Silfor said, "and the metal pins."

"You must hurry," Maelbrigte said. "We'll lose all the skins if the tank empties."

Just for a moment Leon's attention was caught by the back of Torsa's head as he walked through the open gate, a shiny sliver of steel sparkling by his side. But he had no time to think about what it meant, as he turned and ran back towards the forge.

EIGHTEEN

The Fight

The afternoon sun shone low behind Torsa, turning him into a grey silhouette. Doran could hear Rhiannon's sharp breathing next to him. Torsa's body was taut, battle ready. Their eyes met and Doran's mouth ran dry.

On the ground between them, Wolf struggled to hold Pilot down as he tried to stand on his three good legs. The weight of Juniper was helping, pinning Pilot's damaged leg to the floor.

"Wolf," Rhiannon moaned, but she didn't move. Nico hid his face against her thigh.

With one swift movement Torsa raised the sword by its hilt above his head so it hung in front of his face. His eyes flashed at Doran. "You will pay for this with your life."

With an enormous thrust, Torsa strode forward and drove the sword straight through Pilot's chest. "He's no use to me maimed," Torsa spat. Wolf and Juniper sped off in opposite directions as the blade dropped. Doran gasped; his heart clamouring within him. Rhiannon closed her eyes and Nico sobbed.

Trembling, Doran shifted his weight from foot to foot, the dove stone patting against his body reminding him it was there. Fear ran down his spine like a chain. His tongue stuck to the roof of his mouth. "God of Ronin, you are my only hope," he whispered.

Even as he spoke the words, the realisation that he was going to have to stand his ground against Torsa gave him strength. He pulled himself to his full height, balanced his pike in readiness, and looked Torsa in the eye.

Torsa yanked out the sword, holding down Pilot's body with his foot. Pilot groaned for the last time and his final breath passed away. Doran's heart pounded as he watched Torsa slowly bring the heavy sword up level with his ear. The bloodied blade glistened maliciously in the sunlight. Torsa took a step towards Doran. As he did, the sun shone directly into Doran's eyes, blinding him.

Torsa ran forward, swinging the sword, and a shaft of pain shrieked down Doran's arm as the blade glanced off his shoulder, knocking him down. Rhiannon screamed. Doran scrabbled to get to his feet, trying to keep hold of his pike. Torsa kicked it out of his hand, knocking Doran down again. Torsa towered over him, the blade of his sword hanging above Doran's chest.

With a great grunt, Torsa brought the sword down, but

at the last second Doran rolled to one side. The blade narrowly missed him, and sunk deep into the ground. Doran scrambled to his feet, and grabbed his pike with one hand as Torsa bent down to pull the sword from the earth.

"Ronin's God," Doran pleaded, "help me stop him now!" He swung the pike in one swift, desperate movement. The bulbous end caught Torsa in the back of the head, like a hammer blow. Torsa toppled forward, like the felling of a great pine. Doran raised the pike to strike again, but Torsa didn't move.

"He's dead," Nico shouted.

Doran brought the pike's head crashing to the ground in front of Torsa's face. Still he didn't move. "Have I killed him?" he asked, tears running down his face.

Rhiannon dropped to the ground next to Torsa and placed her hand flat on his back. "He breathes," she whispered. "We must bind him now! Quickly!"

Doran's legs began to shake. He fell to his knees beside Rhiannon, tears falling unbidden to the ground. He watched her pull the cord free from her waist. As villagers began to run towards them, she dragged Torsa's arms together and trussed him like a boar, pulling the knots tight with all her might.

Doran sat there, cradling his damaged arm with his good one, rocking backwards and forwards. Nico buried his face against Doran's leg, shaking uncontrollably.

Rhiannon got to her feet and tried to pull Torsa's sword from the ground. Tears slid silently down her cheeks. Doran watched her pulling then yanking it to and fro, wanting to get the sword as far away from Torsa as she could.

"Here let me do it," came a voice from behind her. It was Leon. "It's all right now; we're here."

"He was going to kill him," Rhiannon sobbed. "Leon, I thought Torsa would kill Doran. I thought he was going to kill us all."

The pain down Doran's arm made his head spin. Faces came and went out of focus. "Let me look at the wound," he heard Maelbrigte say kindly. She eased his good hand away from his damaged arm then wrapped it in woollen cloth, tying it around his neck. Immediately the pain eased. "Better?" she asked.

Doran nodded and looked across to the gates – the whole village seemed to have appeared. Torsa had been dragged across to the picket fence and was staring groggily into the distance. Pilot's body lay in a pool of blood in the middle of the earthen road. Governor Erdig and Silfor stood next to each other, frowning.

Rhiannon sat with her arms around Wolf. She smiled and Doran managed to smile back.

"Where's Nico?" he asked.

"He's gone home with Juniper," she replied.

Doran felt for the dove stone and took it out. As his thumb ran over the surface, he felt safe.

"This is a bad business," he heard Governor Erdig say.

"Torsa has to be dealt with," Silfor answered. "We can not let this go on."

Governor Erdig shook his head sadly. "No, indeed. Good warriors defend their neighbours – they don't try to hurt them."

NINETEEN

The Reckoning

"Who killed the dog?" Governor Erdig asked for the third time. The whole village had assembled for the trial. The sharp, familiar smell of the tanning hides drifted across the yard in the silence.

Torsa sat on the hard ground in the middle of the main yard, his arms bound to a post and his legs shackled together. He stared up at Governor Erdig, but said nothing.

Rhiannon sat next to Doran on the step of Governor Erdig's porch. "His arms must ache," she whispered.

Doran nodded. "He's been bound to that post all night."

"My father says it's supposed to break the will."

The whole village watched Governor Erdig walk slowly forward and look down at Torsa. "This feud cannot go on," he said. "We cannot allow you to divide our settlement with your anger. What happened in the past, is in the past. We cannot let feuds tear us apart. They weaken us and make us vulnerable. If you do not promise to stop henceforth, we will banish you."

Rhiannon gasped and swivelled round to look up at her father, who was seated behind her with the other elders. Banishment was the ultimate punishment! She glanced at Doran and then at Leon, who smiled reassuringly at her.

Torsa stared insolently at Governor Erdig and then spat on the ground. Governor Erdig walked back to join the elders, taking his seat at the centre. Rhiannon turned to Doran and placed her hand gently on his arm. It was his turn next.

"Let us all hear what happened," Governor Erdig commanded. "Doran, tell us."

Doran stood up, his arm strapped across his chest in a sling. He held the dove stone tightly in his injured hand. He took a huge breath and said, "Pilot was waiting for us at the gate. He wasn't going to let us past, so Wolf challenged him."

"This has been going on for a while," Rhiannon cut in as she stood up. "Wolf is always wary of Pilot. It's as if he's been expecting a fight."

The crowd murmured and several people nodded. No one, it seemed, trusted Pilot.

"But why did you leave the settlement?" Silfor asked, leaning forward. "Explain yourself Rhiannon. Why did you leave so early yesterday? Where did you go? Who was with you?"

116

Rhiannon turned to look at her father. "Wolf woke me at dawn; he was desperate to get out. When I opened the door he kept pushing me to go with him. Father, I think he knew. He'd been strange since he heard Juniper howling in the night. I followed him through the settlement and that's when I realised Doran and Nico were missing. So we went in search of them – Wolf and me."

Her father did not smile. "Why didn't you come to us for help?"

Rhiannon's face flushed crimson. "I just thought they were late home," she said lamely, looking down at her feet.

"Rhiannon knew about Torsa and me," Doran explained. "She knew he'd been scaring me and taking our fish and our rabbits. She knew I was worried he would hurt Nico. She was worried that I would run away and take Nico with me."

"So, Rhiannon, let me be clear: You set off alone because you thought Doran had run away with Nico?" Governor Erdig asked. His stare bore into her and a sense of shame seemed to wrap itself around her like a cloak. The whole council murmured in shock at her recklessness.

"I took Wolf with me," she stammered. Torsa gave a short snort of contempt. Rhiannon spun round to look at him. "At least Wolf is still alive!" she shouted, holding back her tears. Torsa lifted his head and stared defiantly at the council.

Governor Erdig turned to Doran. "Why didn't you come home when the evening horn sounded yesterday?"

"Nico and I had been working on the allotments. He was tired and hungry, so I sent him home after Miriam. But then Torsa caught him and threatened us both. He terrified

117

Nico saying he'd let Pilot eat him. We tried to get back but Pilot was sitting at the gate. I panicked." Doran clutched at the dove stone and his voice drained away.

Rhiannon placed her hand on his arm. "Tell them about the traps," she said quietly. The whole settlement waited, wanting to understand.

Doran took a deep breath. "For weeks now Torsa has been taking our rabbits. He takes them and then gives them to Pilot to eat while he forces us to watch. So we have nothing to eat. Then on the day of the hunt Pilot brought me down in the woods and if Wolf hadn't saved me he'd have broken my neck. I got up and ran. I didn't know where I was going. When I reached the clearing Torsa fired an arrow at me. I know he hates us because of my family." There was a long pause and then he said, "Pilot would have killed Nico. I could see it in his eyes."

At that point, the leatherman stepped forward and said, "I saw Torsa fighting Doran between the longhouses. I thought it was just the way of young men – but he did have Doran by the throat."

"I saw him firing at Doran at the hunt. I didn't think about it at the time but Torsa would have had time to see it wasn't a boar," another witness added.

Governor Erdig's wife stepped forward, her arms folded tightly across her chest. "Well, I can tell you that Nico is terrified of Torsa. He has nightmares about what will happen to his brother."

Rhiannon thumped back down onto the step and Doran sat next to her. She looked at the dove stone in his hand and the tightness in her chest eased. Behind her, Governor Erdig asked, "Do you have anything to say in your defence, Torsa?"

Torsa sneered contemptuously at them all. "I should have finished them both off," was all he said, and he spat on the ground again.

The council rose and walked into the longhouse to come to a decision. Rhiannon could feel the warmth of Doran at her side. The crowd waited uneasily.

Later that evening, Rhiannon sat looking at her parents' sorrowful faces. The remains of their meal littered the table top between them. Sadness filled Rhiannon and even Wolf's comforting body under her feet could not soften it.

"So, he goes in the morning?" Maelbrigte asked. "Will he take a sword?"

Silfor shook his head. "No. We need our swords, but he has his pike. No dog though; Governor Erdig says he can not have any of the others."

"It was horrible, the way he killed Pilot," Rhiannon said, nodding her head sadly.

"And yet Pilot would have given his life to save him," added Leon.

Silfor put his hand on top of Maelbrigte's and she smiled at him. "Governor Erdig thinks the gods looked after you Rhiannon," he said, "but he thinks you're reckless."

Rhiannon's cheeks reddened in shame and she fiddled with her fingers and sniffed. "I'm sorry," she mumbled, "I didn't mean to be so thoughtless."

"What did Doran mean about meeting a man in the woods?" Leon asked. "Something about a different God?"

Rhiannon fiddled with a piece of bread. She didn't want to talk about Ronin. They wouldn't understand. "There's a man travelling down the river," she said hesitantly, trying to explain. "He's trying to find other members of his tribe because his settlement has been destroyed. He told us about his Father God and how he cares and helps us if we pray to him. Ronin helped Doran feel braver so he didn't run away. He's a good man."

Maelbrigte stared aghast down the table at her daughter. "You met this stranger, and talked to him?" Rhiannon watched her father's hand pat her mother's as it rested on the table.

"He rescued Wolf and me from the river," she blurted out, "when I fell in that time." Maelbrigte looked furiously at her daughter and opened her mouth to speak, but a look from Silfor silenced her.

Leon leaned forward towards her. "Do you believe in this Father God?" he asked.

"Doran does." Rhiannon dragged the dishes towards her, to take them out for washing. She just wanted to hide away. She didn't know what to tell her parents about Ronin. She didn't know what to think. How could she tell her father that perhaps Gobannus didn't exist after all?

"Well, you can never have too many gods," Leon said as he stood up to go and check the forge. "Doran talked of a tribe called Christians. When Governor Erdig asked him to explain, Doran just said he'd prayed to Belisama to help him, but she hadn't listened so he'd talked to this man's God instead." Leon shrugged. "Doran says this Father God gave him strength to stand up to Torsa, even though he was afraid."

"It sounds to me that fear has just unsettled him," Silfor said kindly. "And I thought it was Torsa who had the bang on the head!"

Both parents affectionately watched their son leave the room while Rhiannon stacked the dishes. She kept her eyes on the table as she worked. She didn't know how to explain her newfound trust in Ronin's God.

"I know Torsa was cruel – but he's still a boy. He's no older than Miriam," Maelbrigte said suddenly. "How will he survive alone?"

Silfor leaned back in his chair. "Oh, I suspect he will survive. He'll probably attach himself to one of those travelling bands."

"Oh, Silfor," Maelbrigte replied with a sigh, "what a waste! His father was such a great warrior and protector of us all."

"I know, but we can not keep him here," Silfor replied grimly. "Even his mother agrees. He is selfish and ruthless; who knows how many of us he might have tried to kill? Let's hope he sees sense. Perhaps he will return one day, a better man – a real man – for the experience."

Maelbrigte looked lovingly at Rhiannon. "His poor mother," she said. "What she must be going through, now he's got to leave. Leon is such a gift to us. I'll never moan about him again!"

As Rhiannon left the room she could hear her father chuckling quietly to himself and she laughed inwardly too.

She wondered how long it would be before Leon was in trouble with their mother again.

TWENTY

One Week Later

With a flash of vivid blue the kingfisher plunged into the still water at the long bend in the river. Seconds later up it flew up again, with a small fish trapped in its beak. It landed on a broken branch amongst the twigs and leaves. Rhiannon watched the bird closely. She sat on a boulder, her legs crossed like a pixie on a toadstool. "I wish I was as quick as that bird," she said.

Doran stood in the slow-moving river, with the water swashing around his knees. "You're fast enough." His pike was raised above his shoulder ready to strike a fish as it passed by his feet. The pike was smoother now and rounded at the end, Ronin-style.

"Did you find Ronin?" Rhiannon asked. Doran nodded, his full concentration on catching the fish. "Did you give him his pike back?"

The river lisped as it ran past his legs, its colour a dirty grey. Doran's attention was on the patch of water that his shadow covered. A pair of mallards quacked as they waddled towards them, ignoring Rhiannon as they passed her. Then they straggled noisily onto the river's edge. With a sudden, sharp spring Doran thrust the pike into the water. "Yes!" he said.

"Was he pleased to get it back? Did he ask about me?" Rhiannon asked.

Doran looked at her, vaguely. "What back?"

"His pike."

He smiled. "Oh yes, I took it back to him."

Rhiannon sighed. Shading her eyes with her hand she looked towards the settlement. "It's getting late," she said. "The sun is going down and I'm cold."

"Well, I'm finished here," he said.

Doran pulled his pike from the water. A huge silver fish was skewered through its middle. It briefly thrashed and twitched and then was still. Rhiannon stared. "We can all share that one!" she said, impressed.

"Then let's go home," Doran said, smiling broadly.

Lazily, they walked towards the allotments. The silver fish hung by its gills from the pike over Doran's shoulder as his right hand rested proudly on the hilt of a short knife that hung in its sheath from his belt. "I shall give the salmon to your father."

Rhiannon glanced at him curiously. "Why?"

Doran looked proudly at her. "To thank him for my knife."

Rhiannon smiled. "He'll be pleased."

When they neared the gates, Doran stopped and looked at her. "Yes, he did ask about you," he said.

Rhiannon looked confused. "Who, my father?"

"No, Ronin. I told him about the court and about Torsa being banned. Did you know it wasn't just me Torsa was hurting?" Rhiannon shook her head. "He's been pushing others around, too. It was just that he hated me and my father the most." Doran smiled broadly at her. "I also told him that your parents had banned you from going any further than the stepping stones — and how you're now meant to stay at home and not talk to strangers." Doran couldn't keep the laughter from his voice as he spoke.

Rhiannon snorted. "Only for now," she said impatiently, "until I'm trusted again."

"Ronin said something strange," Doran said. "He said that Jesus the Christ died on a cross. And he said that's why he wears it as a symbol."

The cold wind tugged at Rhiannon's cloak. She pulled it around her more closely to keep herself warm. "The one he wears round his neck?" she asked.

Doran nodded. "According to Ronin, the Romans crucified the Christ and that's why he trusts him."

Rhiannon stopped, looking even more confused. "Why do you trust someone because of the way they died?" she asked. She looked up at the clouds. She couldn't make any sense of it at all.

Doran stopped too. "I don't really understand. It was something to do with him coming to life again. I thought I understood when Ronin explained it but I think I'll ask him again next time I see him. But I do believe his God helped me – I'm sure he did. I think he does care."

Rhiannon nodded. "I think so, too," she said. "Did you find the stone?"

Doran shrugged. "No, I've searched all over but it's gone. Nico swears he hasn't hidden it, but you never know with him. Ronin insists it doesn't matter. The stone didn't do anything; it was just a reminder to pray."

"It looked so like a dove," Rhiannon said, walking on again. "I thought there must be something special about it."

"No, Ronin was definite," Doran replied. "He said none of these things have magical powers: stones, crosses, acorns, none of it. He said what mattered was trust. If you trusted the Father God to help you and you prayed to him then that is all you need."

The pair had been so deep in conversation they hadn't noticed Wolf sitting by the gate waiting for them. His tail had swept an arc of earth behind him. Rhiannon skipped as she saw him and then dropped to one knee so she could hug him as he walked forward to greet her. "He's saved me so many times," she said. She stroked his head then buried her face in the fur of his neck.

"He certainly loves you," Doran said.

"And I him," but her words came out all muffled in fur. "Do you think the dogs knew that Pilot was dangerous?"

"Yes, I do. I think they knew more than we realise. I think Juniper was watching at home and he and Wolf helped us. Who knows where we'd be without them?"

Doran ruffled Wolf's ear. As they turned to walk back through the main yard, Wolf trotted on ahead. "He's getting older," Rhiannon said watching him go.

"He's a faithful friend," Doran said.

Rhiannon smiled at Doran. "That's just what Leon said. He thinks you should train up one of Wolf's pups when they're born. So you've got a dog to hunt with you."

"I'm not sure I could do that," he said.

"You just need to get Wolf to help." Wolf stopped and turned to look back at Rhiannon, his tail wagging lazily behind him. "I tried to tell Leon about Ronin's Father God," Rhiannon added, "but he didn't want to listen. He just said that there were lots of gods and they all have their place. But Belisama didn't help us, did she?"

Doran stopped to lift up his pike, easing the weight of the fish across his shoulder. "I'm going to pray to Father God from now on."

"Me too."

They walked on in silence for a while and then Doran said, "Ronin talked about Torsa. He said that he'd try to find Torsa – to save him."

Rhiannon frowned in confusion. "Save him from what?"

"Ronin didn't say exactly. He just talked about when you're sorry about something you've done and want to change the way you are then the Christ will help you. And that Father God could change Torsa."

Rhiannon snorted. "Did you believe him?"

"It's funny, but when I was there talking to Ronin I did. He seemed so sure. But now I don't know what to think."

Rhiannon shook her head. "I can't see Torsa changing." Then she added briskly, "Mother will expect you tonight for supper if you're giving us that fish."

Doran smiled. "That'll be good! I like your mother's cooking."

As they reached the lane where they parted for their homes, Rhiannon said, "It seems strange that just saying prayers is the right way to get God to help you."

Doran smiled. "I know. I miss having the dove stone, but it doesn't matter. Take the fish. I'll go and get Nico."

If you would like to contact the author about anything you have read in this story, please do so through the contact form on the Dernier Publishing website:

www.dernierpublishing.com

Further study resources can also be found on the website.

Glossary

AUTHOR'S NOTE:

Garrison: A garrison is a place where military troops are stationed.

Hadrian's Wall: When the Roman army was not able to defeat the Scots they built a wall across the north of England to keep the Scots out.

Belisama: When the Roman army invaded Britain they brought with them their religious beliefs. The Romans believed in lots of different gods, all for different occasions and places. Belisama is one goddess whom the Romans worshipped.

Brigantes: The people who lived in the north of England were called Brigantes, long before they were called Lancastrians or Yorkshiremen.

Longhouses: In early Britain bricks and stones were only used to build homes when people were very prosperous. Most homes were made using a rectangular wooden frame panelled by planks and caked in mud. Usually, longhouses would have one room for living in, which would have a fire at one end, and another room for sleeping in; but they could be bigger. Rhiannon's home had a separate kitchen area with stairs to a loft. Governor Erdig's house would be bigger again.

Wild boar: In early Britain, a type of pig lived wild in the countryside which was called a boar. Boars were dangerous if they were cornered or frightened but usually they lived quietly. People hunted them for food until they were all gone.

Pike: A pike is a long, thin wooden stick which is sharpened to a point at one end. It would be used both to hunt with and as a weapon to defend yourself. It was usually just a bit shorter than the person using it and would be home-made.

Allotments: Fences surrounded the groups of homes to protect them from passing thieves and wild animals, but the area outside the fence would be used to grow vegetables. Families would each have their own areas, called allotments.

Monks: These were men who were followers of Jesus so had learned about what it was to be a Christian and who lived lives dedicated to serving others.

CHAPTER 1

Enamelled pins or brooches: Enamelled pins or brooches were made of metal and glass. They were usually highly coloured and used to hold clothing together such as cloaks and shirt openings long before buttons or zips were invented.

Pocket: Early clothing did not have sewn-in pockets like we do today, as they simply had not been thought of. Instead, a pocket was a bag that hung from a belt around the waist.

CHAPTER 2

Torc: A torc is a solid metal neck ring which would almost be a complete circle but would have an opening at the front so you could put it on. Sometimes they would be solid; other times they would be strands of metal, wound together with a round nob, or roundel, at each side of the opening.

Long horns: A horn could be blown to warn members of a settlement in a similar manner that a siren or a car horn might be used today. Sometimes they were made of metal. Sometimes horns were made from sheep's or cows' horns.

Iron awls: Gates were locked by strong bars of wood being drawn along them. These bars ran through iron fittings called awls.

Trestle: A simple wooden table made of planks laid over supports rather than having table legs.

Hoe: This is a flat metal tool with a long wooden handle, used to scrape the surface of the soil. You can use it to remove weeds from between the plants you are growing. People still use hoes in their gardens today.

CHAPTER 3

Forge: A forge is a type of fire that is used to heat metal so that it can be worked to make metal implements such as ploughs and swords. The fire is often made using charcoal so that it will be extremely hot, and it is kept within a grate or basket.

Saxons: These were invaders who set out from northern Europe to conquer Britain. We sometimes call them Anglo-Saxons.

CHAPTER 4

Leatherman: Within settlements people had different roles and tasks. The leatherman would make items such as belts, and bags which hung from them which were used as pockets. They might also make sheaths for knives, and saddles and bridles for horses.

Bellows: Bellows are a device which blow air into a fire to make it burn more strongly. Usually bellows have a wooden handle, which squeezes the air out of a leather bag through a pipe and into the fire.

Gobannus: This is another god the Romans worshipped and brought to Britain. This god was thought to particularly help people who work with metals, who are called blacksmiths today.

Leather gauntlets: These are gloves which come right up to the elbow. They were made from leather and would protect the blacksmiths hands from getting burnt.

Broken scrap: In a small forge, iron would have been recycled from old and broken pieces such as horseshoes and rings for carts and barrels. It would have been important to keep each type of metal separately, so the scrap would have to be sorted.

Scratch awl: This is a tool which a blacksmith – a person who works with metal – would use to make marks on metal surfaces. Sometimes these were light marks to guide other work but often it would be strong marks to decorate whatever was being made.

CHAPTER 5

Longbow: Bows and arrows have been used throughout early history. A longbow is a bow that is almost as tall as a man. It fires arrows with force over long distances.

Training sword: Swords were quite rare items in early history because they were hard to make and very expensive, so not everyone in a settlement could have one. It would still be sensible to train all the people in the settlement in how to use a sword. In this story we have a training sword that was shared.

Ginnel: A ginnel is a northern word for a narrow passageway between two buildings.

CHAPTER 9

Coracle: A small, round light boat, steered with a paddle.

Habit: Monks wore different clothes to everyone else. We call these long, loose clothes *habits*. They were usually tied around the waist with thin rope or twine and often had a hood.

Discussion Questions

CHAPTER 1
Rhiannon is afraid of crossing the river in the dark. What other fears do people have?

CHAPTER 2
Torsa is mean to Doran. How could Torsa explain his nasty behaviour towards him?

CHAPTER 3
Doran and Rhiannon come from very different families. What makes a good family?

CHAPTER 4
The Romans had different gods for each place. Would this be useful to us today?

CHAPTER 5
If we trust God to help us, do we need to know how to defend ourselves?

CHAPTER 6
Rhiannon expects Belisama to help. How do you think prayers are answered?

CHAPTER 7
Doran is afraid of Torsa. How can we avoid being bullied?

CHAPTER 8
Silfor kills the boar. Is the killing of animals ever acceptable today?

CHAPTER 9

Was Rhiannon brave or foolish to approach a stranger?

CHAPTER 10

Ronin is wearing a cross. What do you think this cross means?

CHAPTER 11

Rhiannon has not listened to her parents' advice. How could she explain her actions to them?

CHAPTER 12

Father God answers Rhiannon's prayer for Wolf. Why don't we always get what we pray for?

CHAPTER 13

Doran runs away. Was this the best plan?

CHAPTER 14

Who is the better friend to Doran: Miriam or Wolf?

CHAPTER 15

Ronin likes to pray a lot. Do Ronin and Rhiannon expect Father God to do the same things?

CHAPTER 16

Doran is a coward. Do you agree or disagree?

CHAPTER 17

Leon is always busy working. Why is Leon a good brother?

CHAPTER 18

Was Doran brave or foolish to fight Torsa?

CHAPTER 19

Rhiannon finds it hard to talk to her family about Father God. What makes it difficult to talk to others about God?

CHAPTER 20

Torsa deserves to be banished from the settlement. Do you agree or disagree?

If you enjoyed this book, you may also like:

Deepest Darkness
by Denise Hayward

Abi suffers from terrible nightmares and her life is ruled by her fears. While on holiday in Canada, she makes a new friend who shows her that light shines, even in the deepest darkness. But what difference can the light make?

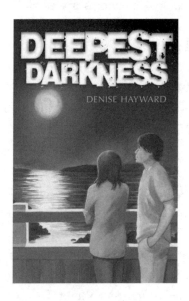

"It is a fantastic adventure and God is really real." - Natalie

"I enjoyed the story very much." - Polina

"This is a brilliant story. It is is one of the best books I've read - EVER!" - Maddie

A Pennyworth of Peppermints
by Mary Weeks Millard

An exciting spy story, set in World War I. Ben and Sidney
find a message in a bottle, washed up on the beach. Is it
just a poem, or is there more to it than meets the eye?

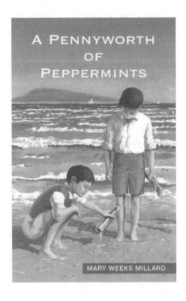

"Cool, interesting, exciting . . . this is a great book!" - Joseph

*"This story is epic . . . it helped me understand what life was
like as a child in the first world war, and reminded me God
is interested in helping us through tough times."* - Florence

Under the Tamarind Tree
by Mary Weeks Millard

Joshua and Timo's lives are about to change for ever. Neither of them want to move to rural Rwanda, but they soon begin some exciting adventures ...

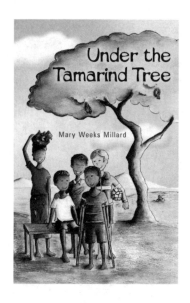

"I just couldn't put it down!" - Hannah

"It shows how God helps us in our lives. I would recommend this book to all my friends." - Jacob